Dig deep into this stocking full of stories and you will find . . .
a wolf who dresses up as Father Christmas, a holly-tree that
gives a precious gift to a very special baby, a plum pudding, a
school Nativity play with a difference and many other delightful
characters to celebrate the wonder and magic of Christmas.

No story has been put in the stocking without very careful
inspection by children's book specialist Pat Thomson. All the
stories are tried and tested favourites, and all by top children's
authors – Eleanor Farjeon, Diana Hendry, Hazel Hutchins,
Geraldine McCaughrean, Catherine Storr and many others.

PAT THOMSON is a well-known author and anthologist.
Additionally, she works as a lecturer and librarian in a teacher
training college – work which involves a constant search for
short stories which have both quality and child-appeal. She is
also an Honorary Vice-President of the Federation of Children's
Book Groups. She is married with two grown-up children and
lives in Northamptonshire.

A
STOCKING
full of
Christmas Stories

COLLECTED BY
PAT THOMSON

ILLUSTRATED BY PETER BAILEY

CORGI BOOKS

A STOCKING FULL OF CHRISTMAS STORIES

A CORGI BOOK 0 552 52739 4

First published in Great Britain by Doubleday, a division of Transworld
Publishers Ltd

PRINTING HISTORY
Doubleday edition published 1992
Corgi edition published 1993

Corgi Books are published by Transworld Publishers Ltd, 61–63
Uxbridge Road, Ealing, London W5 5SA, in Australia by Transworld
Publishers (Australia) Pty. Ltd, 15–25 Helles Avenue, Moorebank, NSW
2170, and in New Zealand by Transworld Publishers (N.Z.) Ltd,
3 William Pickering Drive, Albany, Auckland.

Printed and bound in Great Britain by
Cox & Wyman Ltd, Reading, Berks.

Acknowledgements

The editor and publisher are grateful for permission to include the following copyright stories.

Elizabeth Clark, 'The Cart that kept Christmas' from *Stories to Tell*. Reprinted by permission of Hodder & Stoughton Ltd.

Eleanor Farjeon, 'The Glass Peacock' from *The Little Bookroom* (OUP, 1955). Reprinted by permission of David Higham Associates Ltd.

Diana Hendry, *Christmas in Exeter Street* © 1989 Diana Hendry. Published in the UK by Walker Books Limited. Used with permission.

Hazel Hutchins, 'Wil's Tail', first published in *The Oxford Christmas Story Book* (OUP, 1990). Reprinted by permission of the author.

Geraldine McCaughrean, 'The Rebellious Plum Pudding' first published in *The Oxford Christmas Story Book* (OUP, 1990). Reprinted by permission of the author.

Janet McNeill, 'Ballyutility's Christmas Tree' from *A Pinch of Salt*. Reprinted by permission of Faber & Faber Ltd.

Ruth Manning-Sanders, 'The Christmas Crab Apples' from *Festivals* (Octopus). Reprinted by permission of David Higham Associates Ltd.

Rhoda Power, 'Joseph and the Trees' from *Seven Minute Tales*. Reprinted by permission of Evans Bros., now HarperCollins Publishers Ltd.

Alf Prøysen, 'The Mice and the Christmas Tree' from *Little Old Mrs Pepperpot* (Hutchinson, 1959). Reprinted by permission of Random Century Group.

Joan G. Robinson, 'Teddy Robinson is a Polar Bear' from *Dear Teddy Robinson*, © Joan G. Robinson, 1956, 1960. First published by George G. Harrap & Co.

Catherine Storr, 'Father Christmas' from *The Adventures of Polly and the Wolf*. Reprinted by permission of Faber & Faber Ltd.

Pat Thomson, 'The Cat on the Douvrefell', © 1992 Pat Thomson. Reprinted by permission of the author.

Sylvia Woods, 'While Shepherds Watched' from *Now Then Charlie Robinson* (1987). Reprinted by permission of Faber & Faber Ltd.

Every effort has been made to trace and contact copyright holders before publication. If any errors or omissions occur the publisher will be pleased to rectify these at the earliest opportunity.

CONTENTS

A STOCKING FULL
OF CHRISTMAS STORIES

Christmas in Exeter Street

The day before Christmas Eve, Ben and Jane's grandma and grandpa came to stay at the house in Exeter Street.

It was a lovely old house with big friendly windows, a holly wreath on the front door, and three chimney pots shaped like the crowns of the three wise men.

Ben and Jane's mother, Mrs Maggie Mistletoe, showed Grandpa George and Grandma Ginny where they were to sleep. She had given them the best spare bed-room. This had a big four-poster bed in it. Grandpa George parked his sea boots underneath it and the three cats jumped on to the bed and curled up together.

Grandpa George was a tall old sailor who came in his sea boots. Grandma Ginny came with her knitting and her three cats, One, Two and Three. Wherever Grandma Ginny went her knitting needles went in and out under her elbows and One, Two and Three followed along behind her. Grandpa George and Grandma Ginny brought a Christmas tree.

Ben and Jane's other grandma and grandpa also came to the house in Exeter Street. They were small and skinny and wore their best hats, a woolly bobble hat for Grandpa Angus and a beret with stars on it for Grandma Fanny. Grandma Fanny brought a jar of her special cranberry jelly. Grandpa Angus and Grandma Fanny were given the second-best spare bedroom. This had a small iron bedstead in it. Grandma Fanny said 'This bed is just the right size for two skinnies like us, we can snuggle up together.' Grandpa Angus hung his bobble hat on one knob of the bed and Grandma Fanny hung her star-spangled beret on the other knob of the bed.

Ben and Jane's friends – Amelia, Annie and Amos – arrived on Christmas Eve. Their parents had gone to Timbuktu on Very Important Business and so they came to spend Christmas at the house in Exeter Street. Amelia brought a basket of presents, Annie brought a big Christmas pudding and Amos, who was only three, brought his cuddly blanket and it trailed along behind him like a long, long tail. Mrs Mistletoe took Amelia, Annie and Amos up the stairs to the attic. There they found five beds. Two bunk beds (one for Ben and one for Amos), two mattresses-on-the-floor (for Jane and Annie) and one camp bed with wobbly legs (for Amelia). 'Mind you all hang up your Christmas stockings,' said Mrs Mistletoe. Amos climbed up and down the ladder to the top bunk, trailing his blankie behind him.

Just after supper an unexpected uncle

arrived. It was Uncle Bartholomew back from Australia! Mrs Mistletoe made up a bed for him on the sofa in front of the fire. This was just right for Uncle Bartholomew. Because it had been very hot in Australia he was feeling very chilly; he was so cold he couldn't take off his mittens. Uncle Bartholomew brought a great box of Australian Delight (which was like Turkish Delight, only nicer).

The next to arrive was Mrs Mistletoe's friend Lily, who had nowhere to live. And with Lily came Lily's baby, Lily-Lou. Lily slept on the small sofa in the playroom which had been bounced on so often it was a very funny sagging shape. But this didn't matter because so was Lily. Lily brought home-made Christmas hats, each with a star glued on the front. The kitchen sink was dried out very carefully, then lined with blankets, and Lily-Lou slept in there. Mrs Mistletoe hung Lily-Lou's stocking over the tap. Lily-Lou brought her smile.

Christmas Eve was very stormy and the vicar's roof blew off, so he and his wife and their four children all came to the house in Exeter Street. 'Is there any room in the inn?' asked the vicar, and Mrs Mistletoe said yes, there was. 'We've brought you a carol,' said the vicar and they all stood on the doorstep and sang 'Away in a Manger'. A bed was made up for the vicar and his wife in the bath and a lot of cushions were piled up in the corridor for the four children.

By this time there was quite a lot of noise in the house in Exeter Street and the children next door – Thomas, Tessa and Timothy – came to join the party. They came in their pyjamas and they brought their sleeping bags and their Christmas stockings and they made a camp in the study.

At nine o'clock five aunts came from Abingdon bringing with them a big turkey and their three Pekinese dogs. The aunts – Catherine, Clara, Christabel, Clothilda and Christiana – were very thin ladies so each of them was given a shelf on the dresser in the kitchen and tucked up tightly between the plates and the dangling cups. The Pekinese dogs were packed into shopping baskets and tucked in with dolls' blankets kindly provided by Jane.

At midnight two fat men knocked at the door and asked for a bed for the night because their car had broken down. Each was given a mantelpiece. The first fat man said, 'Please can our wives come in and we will all squash up together on the mantelpiece?' But the wives were very fat, too, and Mrs Mistletoe said she didn't really think two people could fit on one mantelpiece. 'I have two large windowsills to spare,' she said, 'would you like to curl up there?' And the wives said yes please and was there a corner for their five children who were still in the car? Mrs Mistletoe gave a small sigh and said that if Jane and Annie came into her bed, then the five children could sleep on the two mattresses in the attic. The car-children brought an enormous box of crackers.

When everyone was safely tucked up in bed, Mrs Mistletoe counted the number of children asleep in the house in Exeter Street and then she wrote a note for Father Christmas and pinned it on the front door.

No sooner had Mrs Mistletoe got into bed with Jane and Annie than she heard the sound of crying at the front door. She crept down the stairs and looked outside. There on the mat was a small black cat. He brought his snow-white paws. The small black cat slipped inside and found the room where Uncle Bartholomew was asleep on the sofa, dreaming about kangaroos. The small black cat sniffed Uncle

Bartholomew and curled up at his feet.

The last person to arrive at the house in Exeter Street had a lot of trouble with his arithmetic. Father Christmas had to take off his boots and count on his toes to make sure he had remembered all eighteen children. And he had. (Even Lily-Lou.)

On Christmas Day morning they took Lily-Lou out of the sink and Mrs Mistletoe and Jane and Grandpa George peeled a whole sack of potatoes and then they all had a splendid Christmas dinner. They ate the Abingdon aunts' turkey with Grandma Fanny's cranberry jelly and afterwards they had Annie's Christmas pudding. They all wore Lily's Christmas hats (except for Amos who wore his blankie tied round his head because he felt happiest that way) and they pulled the car-children's crackers.

When dinner was over they sat round the fire and ate Uncle Bartholomew's Australian Delight and it was like eating sunshine.

Everyone agreed that the house in Exeter Street was the best place of all to be at Christmas time. The little black cat, curled up in Mrs Mistletoe's lap, thought he might stay until next Christmas and Lily-Lou, snuggled up in Uncle Bartholomew's arms, waved her little curly fingers at the Christmas trees and smiled and smiled and smiled.

This story is by Diana Hendry.

Joseph and the Trees

Which tells why the holly is evergreen and has red berries

The Holy Child was asleep in a manger. Mary, his mother, lay on the ground beside him, with her head pillowed against Joseph's knee, for he had promised to watch over the baby while she rested.

For a few moments Joseph, too, had closed his eyes, and was dreaming of his home in Nazareth, when the baby gave a low cry. Mary stirred in her sleep, and Joseph looked up.

The stable was dark, but a star shone through a long crack in the roof and threw a beam of light across the manger where an ox, an ass, and a horse were pulling away the last wisps of hay. Moving gently, so as not to disturb Mary, Joseph stood up. A little shivering whimper told him that the manger was bare, and that the child had now no soft hay to lie upon and no covering to keep him warm.

With an angry word Joseph drove the animals into the far corner of the stable. 'Could you not have waited until morning?' he asked, striking the ox on the flank. 'See what your greed has done. The child will freeze in the cold.'

The sound of the blow and a long wail of distress from the baby woke Mary. She lifted herself on her elbow. 'Dear Joseph,' she said, 'do not strike the poor beasts. The hay was theirs. If they were too hungry to lend it to us, we have no right to be angry. Give me the child, and I will wrap him in my mantle.'

Still grumbling, Joseph lifted the baby from the manger and put him into Mary's arms.

But the blue mantle, which Mary had spread to dry on the wheel of an old wagon, was of no use. It was still wet with the snow which had been falling when she and Joseph had taken refuge in the stable.

Joseph looked at the shivering child, and his eyes were sad. 'No-one will help us,' he said bitterly. 'The man and his wife would not take us at the inn, and the animals will not lend the hay to warm us and the child. Everyone is against us.'

'No-one is against us,' answered Mary, rocking the baby and looking gently at Joseph. 'The innkeeper and his wife lent us their stable because we were tired and their house was so full that they could not take us in. The animals gave us their manger because there was no cradle for the child. The people and the beasts have helped us, perhaps the trees will be kind, too. Dear Joseph, tell them that we are cold and need some branches for a fire.'

Then Joseph gathered his sheepskin

coat around him, opened the stable door, and went out into the snow.

The ground was white, but the flakes had stopped falling and the air was very clear in the starlight. The gaunt trees stretched their leafless branches towards the sky, and here and there a little icicle hung like a jewel from the end of a twig. There were fig trees and olives, small stunted oaks, and a withered holly. In those days the holly had no red berries and its leaves were not evergreen but fell

14

in the autumn, so that the branches were bare. It looked so shapeless and ugly that Joseph twitched his coat away in disgust when one of its branches caught on the wool. He turned and looked at the fig tree.

'When the sun shines, the fig has so much fruit,' thought Joseph, 'that it will not miss a few dead twigs. I will ask the fig.'

But the fig tree was indignant. 'Do you know what you're asking?' it said.

'Just a few sticks to make a fire for a child who is cold,' pleaded Joseph.

'At all times of the year,' answered the fig tree haughtily, 'my branches lend beauty to the hillside. In the warm weather they are laden with fruit, and the children of Bethlehem rejoice in them. Even when I have no fruit, my silver bark is a joy to all who look at it. Shall this loveliness be burnt for the sake of one child, when so many enjoy it? No, find your sticks elsewhere, old man.'

Distressed and disappointed, Joseph turned away. The air was growing very cold, and he was troubled. He hastened up the hill, searching to right and to left, until he came to a group of olive trees. They looked so soft and lovely in the starlight that he was sure they would help him.

'Trees,' said he, 'in a stable near the inn a little child is dying of cold. He has no fire. Give me, I pray you, a few pieces of your bark for fuel, that I may warm him and his mother.'

'Did you hear that?' shrilled the eldest olive tree, its branches trembling with anger. 'We who give oil and fruit to all the hungry children of Bethlehem are to be stripped of the bark, which keeps us warm, because a strange child is cold. Go back to your own home and get wood.'

'Yes, go back to your own home,' echoed the other olive trees; 'find your fuel there, old man.'

So once again Joseph passed on. He stood before the oaks. 'Will you give a handful of twigs?' he asked; 'there's a child in the stable, and he is crying with the cold. If I do not make him a fire, he will die.'

But the oaks answered roughly, 'Leave us alone. Why should we make ourselves bare and ugly for a stranger, when the children of Bethlehem love us? In the spring they decorate their houses with our leaves, and in the autumn they play with our acorns and oak apples. The more twigs you burn, the fewer leaves

17

and fruit shall we bear. Begone, and find your firewood elsewhere.'

Sadly Joseph retraced his steps.

'Mary was wrong,' he thought. 'All the trees are against us.'

Just at that moment something pulled his sheepskin coat – it was the ugly holly-tree.

'Let *me* help you, Joseph,' it said, 'no-one will miss me, because I am so brown and ugly. I have no fruit for the children to eat or to play with. My leaves are so prickly that no-one picks them to decorate the houses, and they die so soon that they give no beauty to the hillside. This is the only time a child has wanted something which I can give. Take me, Joseph.'

So Joseph loosened the earth around the roots of the holly, and pulling the tree out of the ground, carried it back on his shoulder to the stable: he broke it in pieces and made a fire.

All night long the branches burned with a steady flame, and all night long the stable was warm and the baby slept peacefully. In the morning, when the fire had died down, clusters of scarlet embers glowed in a heap on the ground, and still the stable was warm.

'Poor little holly-tree!' said Joseph; 'there is nothing left.'

'Happy little holly-tree!' said Mary; 'it has warmed the Christ-child. Because of this every holly-tree all the world over shall have leaves that are always green and berries as red as the embers of this fire. And when children remember the Christ-child's birthday, they will make their homes beautiful with holly.'

Ever since that night the holly has been an evergreen with berries red as fire, and people bring it home at Christmas.

This story is by Rhoda Power.

19

Ballyutility's Christmas Tree

Maybe you know the village of Bally-utility. If you've been through it in the train you must have noticed the tidy back gardens, all planted out with orderly potatoes and plump cabbages – there isn't a square inch of ground wasted or a pod of peas that could hold another pea. If you go through the single street you'll find there isn't much in the way of front gardens – most of the houses just have a little square of gravel, except the house at the corner where there is a straggling fir tree. You won't find any children playing in the street either – they've generally got something better to do, and nobody whistles, except to call up a dog. Nobody sings either, except the children in the school, and that's a lesson, so it's different. And when a stranger goes by the dogs take it in turns to bark. That's what it's like in Ballyutility.

Or rather that's what it was like. But something happened last Christmas in Ballyutility, and that's what I want to tell you about. Early in December if you'd gone through the village you'd hardly have known what month it was. You might have heard the children in the school practising carols for the Boxing Day Concert in aid of the Deserving Poor, but there wasn't any sign of Christmas to be seen in any of the three shop windows – the Grocer, the Chemist or the Post Office. Everyone was busy in Ballyutility, but then everybody always was. Mr Jamison, the Grocer, was perhaps the busiest of all – he certainly thought he was. But he didn't festoon his shop with paper chains just because

22

Christmas was coming, nor did he spread it over with artificial frost, or put blobs of cottonwool hanging on strings down the window to look like snow. It wasn't that he didn't know all about these things, for when he was a boy Mr Jamison was apprenticed to his uncle who had a grocer's shop in Belfast, and the week before Christmas his uncle and he had stayed late night after night, sticking blobs of cottonwool on bits of string, till the window was a whirling fairyland, and neither of them grudged the time they spent at it or the clearing up afterwards. But since he had set up shop for himself in Ballyutility Mr Jamison had changed. 'A shop's a shop, not a scene out of a pantomime,' he said. So though the window was full of raisins and sultanas and currants, of candied peel and almonds, of cherries and preserved ginger, of nutmeg and cinnamon and spice and icing sugar, they all sat in their packets in neat and tidy rows, and there wasn't a cottonwool snowflake or a sprig of holly to be seen.

While Mr Jamison was busy making money in his shining shop Mrs Jamison was busy in her shining house, bringing up Anna and Effie and Jane and little Ben. Effie and Jane and little Ben had just got over the whooping cough, and what with wrapping them up in extra warm mufflers every time they went out and unwrapping them again every time they came in, she had been busier than usual. Perhaps that was why she didn't notice how much of her time Anna was spending in the house next door. Mrs McIlvenny and Hughie lived in the house next door – it was the corner house, the one with the fir tree outside it – and Anna and Hughie were the same age, and had always been great friends. But Hughie had spent a year in a hospital in Belfast and was just home and had a couple of months yet to lie in bed.

A couple of days before Christmas Mrs Jamison went into her back garden to hang out her dishcloths and found Mrs McIlvenny doing the same thing in hers. 'How's Hughie keeping today?' asked Mrs Jamison, taking the last of the clothes-pegs out of her mouth.

'He's coming on,' said Mrs McIlvenny, 'but it's not a thing you can hurry. Your Anna is up in the room with him now.'

'Is that where Anna is?' said Mrs Jamison, rather vexed. 'She slipped off when she had the dishes done, and I don't believe she has her lessons half learned. Will you call her down for me?'

'Ah, don't call her down,' Mrs McIlvenny begged, 'Hughie's always extra glad to see Anna. She helps him to put in his time.'

'It seems a sin to have that much time to waste,' Mrs Jamison said, and suddenly wondered what she was thinking of, wasting her own time gossiping over the garden fence. There was plenty to do in the house without this. So she hurried indoors and took out her knitting, and was soon busy on the pair of gloves she was making for little Ben's Christmas present. The pattern book she was using said white fluffy wool with scarlet rabbits embroidered on them, but Mrs Jamison was doing them in grey, which was much more serviceable, and leaving out the rabbits. Even little Ben had enough sense to know that rabbits weren't scarlet! So she sat and knitted, making the needles click and dance up and down the rows, and listened to Effie and Jane murmuring and whooping over their homework, and she wished Anna would come home instead of wasting her time next door with Hughie McIlvenny.

But Anna wasn't wasting her time; she was sitting on the end of Hughie's bed, with her schoolbag on her knee, and the two of them were very busy indeed.

'See what I've brought for you today,' said Anna, taking some great plump fir-cones out of her bag. 'I juked in at the minister's gate on my way home from school. There's hundreds of them just lying about on the grass.'

'Those are grand,' said Hughie, 'but there's only a wee lick of the silver paint left at the bottom of the bottle. What else have you got, Anna?'

She dived into the bag again. 'Here's the tops off the lemonade bottles from the shop. If we hang them in long strings they'll turn in the wind, and the lights will shine on them.'

'They'll be like strings of stars,' Hughie cried. 'What else have you?'

'Silver paper from tangerines, and gold paper off the vinegar bottles,' Anna said, smoothing the shining sheets lovingly, 'but wait till you see here! Easy, Hughie, you'll have them broken.'

'What is it?' Hughie breathed, his eyes alight.

'The electric fused at the Bible Class on Wednesday, and when Mr Simpson was changing the bulbs I got him to give me the duds. You could paint them up with shiny paint, couldn't you, Hughie?'

'They had real lights that lit up on the Christmas tree at the Hospital,' said Hughie, 'green lights and blue lights and red lights. I wish we had real lights.'

'It's no good wishing,' Anna said stoutly, 'but if I fix my bicycle lamp at the bottom of the tree it'll throw its light up through the branches. And there'll be the light from the street lamp, and the light from your room.'

'Did you bring *Her*?' Hughie asked.

'I did. Here she is,' said Anna, tenderly unwrapping the tissue paper from her last package, 'look Hughie!'

Hughie gasped. 'My – oh! Isn't she grand? Why do you never play with her, Anna?'

'Mother says dolls are a waste of time,' Anna answered; 'it was my auntie from Belfast that bought her for me – the same auntie that gave me the yellow beads. I never got wearing them either. Mother put them away.'

'She's a beauty,' said Hughie, taking the doll carefully in his hands, 'I'll make her wings and a little wand, and a silver crown for her hair.'

'Oh Hughie,' cried Anna, in sudden distress, 'I've just thought! What'll we do if it rains? Look at her lovely curly hair! She'll be ruined!'

'It'll not rain,' Hughie said, lying back again on his pillows, for he was tired with the excitement, 'it couldn't rain on Christmas Eve.'

Hughie was right, it didn't rain. Christmas Eve was fine and still and starlit. But the shops shut at their usual time in Ballyutility, for everyone had made shopping lists, and had bought their presents long ago. There were no carol singers about either, because the school children were to sing their carols at the Boxing Day Concert (in aid of the Fund for the Deserving Poor) so there wasn't any need for them to sing them twice, was there? Ballyutility village street was deserted, everyone was indoors having their tea or tying up their presents with brown paper and string – brown paper that would come in useful for parcels afterwards – so no-one saw Anna Jamison when she came cautiously out of her back door, carrying her mother's step-ladder.

Half an hour later the schoolmistress, who had not lived long enough in Bally-utility to be as clever at arranging her Christmas as everyone else, stepped out into the street to post a Christmas card to an aunt whom she had forgotten about. But no sooner had she stepped out than she stepped back again, and called to Tommy, her landlady's little boy, who was cleaning the shoes in the scullery to 'come and look'.

'I declare to goodness,' said Tommy wonderingly, as he stood in the door-way with the blacking brushes still in his hands, 'I declare to goodness – it's – a Christmas Tree.'

'Come on in out of that, Tommy,' his mother called, 'what are you standing there for? There's a whole pile of shoes waiting on you.'

'This is one night they may wait,' declared Tommy, and banging down the brushes he was away out into the street, hatless and coatless, knocking on Mrs Jamison's door.

'Come on,' he cried, hammering on the door with his fists, 'come on till you see! Effie! Jane! Come on out, the whole lot of you. The tree! The tree!'

'Come back!' called Mrs Jamison, as Effie and Jane ran out to look, leaving the door wide open behind them, 'come back at once. Effie! Jane! You'll catch your death.'

But it was no use telling them to come back. For they were away – to stand – and gaze – and run and knock on other doors,

and bring more wondering children to see the fir tree, transformed in all its fantastic finery, jewelled and adorned, and magically lit by the bicycle lamp, the street lamp, and the light that poured down from Hughie's bedroom. And Hughie from his window was looking down on a flower-bed of children's faces, upturned to the tree, fringed by a crowd of anxious mothers who had followed them out with coats and scarves.

'All those strings of shining stars,' declared one child, as the wind set the lemonade tops swinging and turning, 'as many stars as there are in the sky.'

'What a lot of time it must have taken,' said his mother who was standing behind him, 'and what a waste of time too!'

'What a waste!' echoed the children dutifully.

'Silver fir cones,' cried a little girl, 'just as if they were all covered with frost. Look how beautifully they sparkle!'

'What a waste of paint!' declared her

mother, and the children breathed again in chorus. 'What a waste! What a waste!'

'Would you look at the fairy at the top!' piped up the smallest girl of all, 'golden wings she has! And a crown! And look at her lovely hair!'

'If it rains,' said her mother, 'her hair will be ruined. What a waste! It will all be wasted!'

'What a waste!' cried the children all together, 'what a lovely waste! What a lovely, *lovely* waste!'

Then they were all very quiet. Someone in the back row called out, 'Here's Mr Jamison coming!' and everybody stood back a little to let Mr Jamison through.

'A crowd in the streets at this time of night!' he declared. 'These children ought to be in their beds. What's it all about? What sort of a carry-on's this? A tree! A Christmas tree!'

'Isn't it lovely, Mr Jamison?' said the smallest girl of all, without taking her eyes off the tree. 'Look at those stars – and the fairy at the top.'

Mr Jamison stood and looked. Then he said slowly, 'It needs the snow. That's what it needs – the snow.'

One boy at the back, who was bolder than the others, piped up:

> Good King Wenceslas looked out
>   On the Feast of Stephen,
> When the snow lay round about
>   Deep and crisp and even.

And before he had finished the verse they were all singing with him.

So Ballyutility had its Christmas Eve – and its Christmas, too. Little Ben Jamison, who had slept through all the excitement, was taken out by his big sister Anna on Christmas morning. Anna was wearing her yellow beads, and first he pulled at these, but when he saw the tree he crowed and chuckled and clapped his hands which were fine and warm in the new gloves his mother had given him (with scarlet rabbits on the backs – his mother had sat up very late when she went in from the Christmas tree the night before). Although there were now no lights on the tree it looked just as lovely, for it was covered with cascades of cottonwool snow from head to foot. (Mr Jamison had knocked up the chemist and bought all the cottonwool in the shop, and he had gone to bed very late too.)

If you try to visit Ballyutility now you won't be able to find it because they've changed the name of the place. The new name was in the paper the other day; they'd won a prize for the best display of flowers in the village street. The new name is much nicer than the old one was. They chose it just because they liked the sound of it. It's a beautiful name, but it doesn't mean a thing.

This story is by Janet McNeill.

Father Christmas

One day Polly was in the kitchen, wash-
ing currants and sultanas to put in a
birthday cake, when the front door bell
rang.

'Oh dear,' said Polly's mother, 'my
hands are all floury. Be a kind girl, Polly,
and go and open the door for me, will
you?'

Polly was a kind girl, and she dried
her hands and went to the front door.
As she left the kitchen, her mother called
after her.

'But don't open the door if it's a wolf!'

This reminded Polly of some of her
earlier adventures, and before she opened

the door, she said cautiously, through the letter box, 'Who are you?'

'A friend,' said a familiar voice.

'Which one?' Polly asked. 'Mary?'

'No, not Mary.'

'Jennifer?'

'No, not Jennifer.'

'Penelope?'

'No. At least I don't think so. No,' said the wolf decidedly, 'not Penelope.'

'Well, I don't know who you are then,' Polly said. 'I can't guess. You tell me.'

'Father Christmas.'

'*Father Christmas?*' said Polly. She was so much surprised that she nearly opened the front door by mistake.

'Father Christmas,' said the person on the doorstep. 'With a sack full of toys. Now be a good little girl, Polly, and open the door and I'll give you a present out of my sack.'

Polly didn't answer at once.

'Did you say Father Christmas?' she asked at last.

'Yes of course I did,' said the wolf loudly. 'Surely you've heard of Father Christmas before, haven't you? Comes to good children and gives them presents and all that. But not, of course, to naughty little girls who don't open doors when they're told to.'

'Yes,' Polly said.

'Well, then, what's wrong with that? You know all about Father Christmas and

I'm pretending to be – I mean, here he is. I don't see what's bothering you and making you so slow.'

'I've heard of Father Christmas, of course,' Polly agreed. 'But not in the middle of the summer.'

'Middle of the what?' the wolf shouted through the door.

'Middle of the summer.'

There was a short silence.

'How do you know it's the summer?' the wolf asked argumentatively.

'We're making Mother's birthday cake.'

'Well? I don't see what that has to do with it.'

'Mother's birthday is in July.'

'Perhaps she's rather late in making her cake?' the wolf suggested.

'No, she isn't. She's a few days early, as a matter of fact.'

'You mean it's going to be her birthday in a day or two?'

'You've got it, Wolf,' Polly agreed.

'So we're in July now?'

'Yes.'

'It's not Christmas?'

'No.'

'Not even if we happened to be in Australia? They have Christmas in the summer there, you know,' the wolf said persuasively.

'But not here. It's nearly half a year till Christmas,' Polly said firmly.

'A pity,' the wolf said. 'I really thought I'd got you that time. I must have muddled up my calendar again – it's so confusing, all the weeks starting with Mondays.'

Polly heard the would-be Father Christmas clumping down the path from the front door; she went back to the currants.

The weeks went by; Mother's birthday was over and forgotten, holidays by the sea marked the end of summer and the beginning of autumn, and it was not until the end of September, when the leaves

41

were turning yellow and brown, and the days were getting shorter and colder, that Polly heard from the wolf again. She was in the sitting-room when the telephone bell rang; Polly lifted the receiver.

'I ont oo thpeak oo Folly,' a very muffled voice said.

'I'm sorry,' Polly said, politely, 'I really can't hear.'

'Thpeak oo FOlly.'

'I still can't quite hear,' Polly said.

'I ont oo – oh BOTHER these beastly whiskers,' said quite a different voice. 'There, now can you hear? I've taken bits of them off.'

'Yes, I can hear all right,' Polly said puzzled. 'But how can you take off your whiskers?'

'They weren't really mine. I mean they're mine, of course, but not in the usual way. I didn't grow them, I bought them.'

'Well,' Polly asked, 'how did you keep them on before you took them off?'

'Stuck them on with gum,' the voice replied cheerfully. 'But I haven't taken that bit off yet. The bit I took off was the bit that goes all round your mouth. You know, a moustache. It got awfully in the way of talking, though. The hair kept on getting into my mouth.'

'It sounded rather funny,' Polly agreed. 'But why did you have to put it on?'

'So as to look like the real one.'

'The real what?'

'Father Christmas, of course, silly. How would I be able to make you think I was Father Christmas if I didn't wear a white beard and all that cotton woolly sort of stuff round my face, and a red coat and hood and all that?'

'Wolf,' said Polly solemnly – for of course it couldn't be anyone else – 'Do you mean to say you were pretending to be Father Christmas?'

'Yes.'

'And then what?'

'I was going to say if you'd meet me

at some lonely spot – say the crossroads at midnight – I'd give you a present out of my sack.'

'And you thought I'd come?'

'Well,' said the wolf persuasively, 'after all I look exactly like Santa Claus now.'

'Yes, but I can't see you.'

'Can't See Me?' said the wolf, in surprise.

'We can't either of us see each other. You try, Wolf.'

There was a long silence. Polly rattled the receiver.

'Wolf!' she called. 'Wolf, are you there?'

'Yes,' said the wolf's voice, at last.

'What are you doing?'

'Well, I was having a look. I tried with a small telescope I happened to have by me, but I must admit I can't see much. The trouble is that it's so terribly dark in there. Hold on for a minute, Polly. I'm just going to fetch a candle.'

Polly held on. Presently, she heard

a fizz and a splutter as the match was struck to light the candle. There was a long pause, broken by the wolf's heavy breathing. Polly heard him muttering: 'Not down there . . . Try the other end then . . . Perhaps if I unscrew this bit . . . Let's see this bit of wire properly . . .'

There was a deafening explosion, which made poor Polly jump. Her ear felt as if it would never hear properly again. Obviously the wolf had held his candle too near to the wires and something had exploded.

'I do hope he hasn't hurt himself,' Polly thought, as she hung up her own receiver. 'It sounded like an awfully loud explosion.'

She saw the wolf a day or two later in the street. His face and head were covered with bandages, from amongst which one eye looked sadly out.

'Oh Wolf, I am so sorry,' said kind Polly, stopping as he was just going to pass her. 'Does it hurt very much? It must have been an awfully big explosion.'

'Explosion? Where?' said the wolf, looking eagerly up and down the street.

'Not here. At your home. When you rang me up the other day.'

'Oh that!' said the wolf airily. 'That wasn't really an explosion. Just a spark or two and a sort of bang, that's all. I just got the candle in the way of the wires and they melted together, or something. Nothing to get alarmed about, thank you, Polly.'

'But your face,' Polly said, 'the bandages. Didn't you get hurt in that explosion?'

'No. But that gum! Whee-e-e-w! I'll tell you what, Polly,' the wolf said impressively. 'Don't ever try and stick a beard or whiskers on top of where your fur grows, with spirit gum. It goes on all right, but getting it off is – well! If it had been my own hair it wouldn't have been more painful getting it off. Next time I'm going to have one of those beards on sort of spectacle things you just hook over your ears. Don't you think that would be better?'

'Much better.'

'Not so painful to take off?'

'I should think not,' Polly agreed.

'Well you just wait till I've got these bandages off,' the wolf said gaily, 'and then you'll see! My own mother wouldn't know me.'

Perhaps it took longer than Polly expected to grow wolf fur again: at any rate it was a month or two before Polly heard from the wolf again, and she had nearly forgotten his promise, or threat, of coming to find her. It was just before Christmas, and Polly was out with her mother doing Christmas shopping. The streets were crowded and the shop windows were gay with silver balls and frosted snow. Everything sparkled and shone and glowed, and Polly held on to Mother's hand and danced along the pavements.

'Polly,' said her mother. 'Would you like to go to the toy department of Jarold's? I've got to get one or two small things there, and you could look round. I think they've got some displays of model railways and puppets, and they generally have a sort of Christmas fair with Father Christmas to talk to.'

Polly said yes, she would very much, and they turned in at the doors of the enormous shop and took a luxuriant gilded lift up to the third floor, to the toy department. It really was fascinating. While her mother was buying coloured glass balls for the Christmas tree, and a snowstorm for Lucy, Polly wandered about and looked at everything. She saw trains and dolls and bears; she saw puzzles and puppets and paperweights. She saw bicycles, tricycles, swings and slides, boats and boomerangs and cars and carriages. At last she saw an archway, above which was written 'Christmas Tree Land'. Polly walked in.

There was a sort of scene arranged in the shop itself, and it was very pretty. There were lots of Christmas trees, all covered with sparkling white snow, and the rest of the place was rather dark so that all the light seemed to come from the trees. In the distance you could see reindeer grazing, or running, and high snowy mountains and forests of more Christmas trees. At the end of the part where Polly was, sat Father Christmas on a sort of throne. There was a crowd of children round him and a man in ordinary clothes, a shop manager, was encouraging their mothers to bring them up to Father Christmas so that they could tell him what they hoped to find in their stockings or under the tree on Christmas Day.

Polly drew near. She thought she would tell Father Christmas that what she wanted more than anything else in the world was a clown's suit. She joined a line of children waiting to get up to the throne.

The child in front of Polly was frightened. She kept on running out of line back to her mother, and her mother kept on putting her back in her place again.

'I don't want to go and talk to that Father Christmas,' the little girl said, 'he isn't a proper Father Christmas.'

'Nonsense,' her mother said sharply. 'Don't be so silly. Stand in that line and go up and tell him what you want in your stocking like a nice little girl.'

The little girl began to cry. Polly, looking sharply at Father Christmas couldn't help rather agreeing with her. Father Christmas had the usual red coat and hood and a lot of bushy white hair all over his face. But somehow his manner wasn't quite right. He certainly asked the children questions, but not in the pleasantest tone of voice, and his reply to some of their answers was more of a snarl than a promise.

The little girl in front of Polly was

finally persuaded to go up and say something in a breathy, awestruck whisper. Polly, just behind her, was near enough to hear the answer.

'Box of sweets,' said Father Christmas in a distinctly unpleasant tone. 'What do you want a box of sweets for? You're quite fat enough already to satisfy any ordinary person, I should think.'

The child clutched her mother's hand tightly, and the manager who was standing near, looked displeased. 'Come,

come,' Polly heard him say sharply in Father Christmas's ear, 'you can do better than that, surely.'

Father Christmas jumped, threw a sharp glance over his shoulder at the manager and leant forward to the little girl. 'Yes, of course you shall have a box of sweets,' he said. 'Only wouldn't you like something more interesting? For instance a big juicy steak, with plenty of fried potatoes? Or what about pork chops? I always think myself there's nothing like . . .'

'Next please,' the manager called out loudly. 'And a happy Christmas to you, dear,' he added to the surprised little girl who was being led away by her mother, unable to make head or tail of this extraordinary Father Christmas.

Polly moved up. The Father Christmas inclined his ear towards her to hear what she wanted in her stocking, but Polly had something else to say.

'Wolf, how could you!' she hissed in a horrified whisper. 'Pretending to be

Father Christmas to all these poor little children – and you're not doing it at all well, either.'

'It wasn't my fault,' the wolf said, gloomily. 'I never meant to let myself in for this terrible affair. I just put on my costume – and I did the beard rather well this time, don't you think? – and I went out to see if I could find you, and this wretched man' – and he threw a glance of black hate at the shop manager – 'nobbled me in the street, and pulled me in here, and set me to asking the same stupid question of all these beastly children. And they all want the same things,' he added venomously. 'If it's boys they want space guns, and if it's girls they want party frocks and television sets. Not one of them's asked for anything sensible to eat. One of them did ask for a baby sister,' he said thoughtfully, 'but did she really want her to eat, I ask myself?'

'I should hope not,' Polly said firmly.

'And I'm much too hot and my

whiskers tickle my ears horribly,' the wolf complained. 'And there's not a chance of snatching a bite with this man standing over me all the time.'

'Wolf, you wouldn't eat the children!' Polly said in protest.

'Not all of them,' the wolf answered. 'Some of them aren't very—'

'Next please,' said the manager loudly. A deliciously plump juicy little boy was pushed to stand just behind Polly. He was reciting to himself and his mother, 'I want a gun, an' I want soldiers, an' I want a rocking 'orse, an' I want a steam engine, an' I want . . .'

'I think you're going to be busy today,' Polly said, 'I probably shan't be seeing you for a time. Happy Christmas,' she added politely, as she made way for the juicy little boy. 'I hope you enjoy yourself with all these friendly little girls and boys.'

'Grrrrrr,' replied Father Christmas. 'I'll enjoy myself still more when I've unhooked my beard and got my teeth into one unfriendly little girl. Just you wait, Polly: Christmas or no Christmas, I'll get you yet.'

This story is by Catherine Storr.

The Cart that kept Christmas

It was Christmas Eve and it was a cold and frosty day. The hedges were white, the roads were hard, the fields looked grey instead of green, and the sky was dark. The only thing that did not look pinched and shivery was the new little red house with a roof of bright red tiles that stood in a square patch of ground with a thorn-hedge all round it.

The little red house – it was really a bungalow – belonged to Jim the Carrier. Jim was not really a Carrier any longer, though everyone still called him so. For twenty, thirty, forty years Jim and his black cart with a covered top and his strong horse Brownie had gone to and fro, to and fro, twice every week from the village on the hill to the town in the hollow. Up hill and down dale they went, bringing butter and eggs and chickens and bacon from the village; carrying back parcels for the Squire and toys and sweets and candles, matches and sugar and currants and flour – everything you can think of, for the village shop – and people too who had gone to town to buy or to visit their friends. They all came jogging back in Jim the Carrier's Cart at the end of the day.

But now Jim had retired. He was growing old. So was Brownie and so was the Cart. Jim had saved a little money and his old aunt had left him some more. He had bought a bit of ground, and his cousin who had a brickfield had given him bricks and tiles. Another cousin who was a bricklayer had come to help him build. They put up the little red bungalow and a shed for Brownie to shelter in on cold or rainy days.

Part of the field was left for Brownie and the part near the bungalow was made into a garden. There were vegetables at the back and sides and flower-beds in front, and roses and creepers were planted against the house. Jim had worked hard that summer; he was proud of his house and garden and Brownie was happy in his field.

But you may have noticed that I have said nothing about the Cart. The old Carrier's Cart was not happy at all. There seemed to be no place for it and no use for it any more. When Jim moved into his new house the Cart had come creaking up the lane behind Brownie with Jim's bit of furniture in it. The lane was rough and the load was heavy and once when the Cart bumped over a big stone there was a loud creak and a crack. Jim shook his head and said, 'I'm afraid that back axle's broken' (the axle is the bar of wood that goes between the wheels).

When the Cart was unloaded they

found it was true. The axle was cracked right across. If it broke, the wheels would come off and the Cart would go *bump* in the road.

Now that Jim was Carrier no longer he did not need a Cart and it was too old to sell. So it had never been mended; it just stood in a corner of Jim's garden by the hedge with its shafts trailing on the ground. The rain beat on it and the wind tugged at it and the sun faded it as the months went by. It felt old and shabby and lonely.

It was feeling particularly unhappy this Christmas Eve. Jim had shut Brownie up in his shed with some hay to munch and a good bed of dry bracken fern to keep him snug. The Cart heard him say, 'Well, old fellow, this is a bit different to last Christmas Eve, ain't it!' And then he had gone into the house and lit the lamp and poked the fire and sat down to his tea. Jim was very happy and comfortable and so was Brownie, but the Cart was not. It did not mind being cold – carts are used to that, of course – but it did mind being empty.

'Different to last Christmas,' said the Cart to itself, creaking sadly in the frost, 'indeed, I should think it *is*!' It thought of the busy, cheerful days when it went to town with Jim and Brownie, feeling clean and smart with its black tarred hood. There was a good smell of butter and bacon and plenty of chat when they stopped by the roadside to pick up parcels and people from cottages and farms; and there were the oddest and most interesting parcels when they jogged home again and everyone had plenty to tell of all they had seen and heard in the shops and inns.

Now the Cart stood all alone by the side of the hedge and no-one came near it. Jim looked at it sometimes and said, 'Don't know what to do about the old Cart; it seems a shame to chop it up and burn it.' He had been too busy to think much about it. It was certainly a very dull life for the Cart.

The old Cart was not the only one who was feeling cold and lonely that Christmas Eve. The little brown hen who was creeping along the lane was feeling cold and lonely too, and she was frightened as well. She had lost her way and lost her home and lost her friends. She did not know what to do.

She belonged to a farm about two miles away. The farm stood in a very quiet road where few people came. The little brown hen – who was not quite two years old – had never seen a motor car till that morning. She had been happily pecking and scratching in the road with all her friends, among some straw that had fallen from a cart, when suddenly a car came snorting round the corner. All the hens said, 'Cuk-cuk-cuk-cuk-*cuk*,' and flew this way and that into the hedge. But our little hen, who was more

frightened than any of them, flew flapping and shrieking down the road in front of the car.

She was too frightened to stop, the road was narrow and the hedges were high. The car seemed like a terrible monster chasing her. On and on she went. The driver was far too kind to go over her and he could not get past her. If he stopped, the little brown hen stopped too, running backwards and forwards, quite muddled and distracted. So on they went, uphill and uphill, till suddenly the lane turned, and just at the turning was a gate. It was right in front of the little brown hen. She gave one loud 'Cuk–cuk–cuk,' and flapped her wings and flew over the gate.

The driver said 'Thank goodness!' and hurried on, and the little brown hen hurried too. She scurried across the field and through the hedge because she was quite sure the car was still behind her. She went scuttling across the field beyond, and stopped quite suddenly in the middle and said to herself in surprise, 'Dear me! there's nobody there!' Then she began to peck and scratch very busily, because she was hungry after running so fast.

But the ground was frozen hard. There was not a worm to be found; even the grass was stiff with frost. The hen soon stopped pecking and began to think about finding her way home. She looked about. She was in the middle of a large field with a thorn-hedge all round it. There was no path and she did not know which way she had come. There was nobody at all to tell her which way to go. The rabbits were in their burrows; the birds were tucked up in the hedges sheltering from the frost. Everything was perfectly still; even the rooks were humped in the tree-tops, too cold and sleepy to caw.

The hen gave a sad little cluck and began to walk slowly across the field. She found a hole in the hedge and strayed across the next field, looking anxiously about to see if she was getting near home. She crossed one field after another and all the time, though she did not know it, she was going farther away from her family and friends with every step she took.

At last, late in the afternoon when it was growing dusk, she found herself in a lane with high ragged hedges on either side. She was very cold and hungry by that time and she was pleased to find the lane; it seemed more friendly and familiar than the wide bare fields and it was sheltered too. She scratched about among the fallen leaves and found two beetles and a slug which comforted her very much. Then she pattered on and presently she came to a gate and path.

'Crr–rr–rr,' said the little hen, 'this looks like home,' and she scuttled under the gate.

It was not her home, of course; that was two miles away. As perhaps you have guessed, it was Jim the Carrier's new little house. But the hen was so cold and tired that she was ready to shelter anywhere that seemed safe and friendly. She pattered carefully about the little garden till she came to the corner where the old Cart stood.

'That looks a good place to sleep,' said the little hen, and she gave a jump and a flutter up to the place where Jim used to sit in the front of the Cart and she peeped inside. It was dark and it was empty, but there was a kind of comfortable feeling about it and there was still a good smell of bacon and butter and people, which was very comforting to a poor lost little hen.

She gave a cautious little cluck-cluck and hopped inside.

You cannot imagine how happy and pleased the old Cart felt. It was going to have company at last! It kept perfectly quiet; it was afraid even to creak. The hen's little feet pattered over the floor till she came to the very farthest corner. The Cart knew what she would find there – a little drift of dry leaves, birch leaves, hazel leaves and hawthorn leaves. The wind had twisted and twirled and tossed them this way and that, when they were red and brown and golden in the autumn, and at last they had fluttered under the hood of the Cart and there they lay in a warm dry crackling bed, all ready for the little brown hen.

'Chuck-chuck-chuck-*chuck*,' said the hen contentedly, and she settled down among the leaves, tucked her head under her wing and went fast asleep. The old Cart was very contented too. It had someone to shelter; there was a snug and comfortable feeling about it that it had missed for very many days.

It snowed hard in the night, that Christmas Eve. When Jim woke up on Christmas morning, everything was white. He went out before he had his breakfast to give Brownie another armful of hay and some sugar because it was Christmas Day. 'Merry Christmas, old boy,' said Jim.

He tramped round the garden and looked at his cabbages all furry with snow, and at his flower-beds tucked up tidily under a snow-white counterpane with neat red edgings of tiles. The old Cart had a white top to its black hood and white trimmings to its wheels. Jim stopped a minute to look at it and gave it a friendly bang on the side: 'Merry Chris . . .' said Jim, but before he could finish there came the most surprising noise:

'Crack-cra-cra-cuck-cuck-cuck-cra-cra-cra-*cuk*,' shrieked the brown hen, and out of the Cart she flapped and flew. She fluttered into the snow and stood there with her beak wide open and her head in the air, making more noise than you would think one small hen could possibly manage.

Jim looked at her and scratched his head. 'I don't know where you came

from, old lady,' he said, 'but I think I'll have a look inside the Cart and see what you've been doing.'

He climbed up and looked, and there, lying on a snug nest of brown dry leaves, was a beautiful warm brown egg!

'*Well!*' said Jim to the Cart, 'there's a nice Christmas present that you and the hen have given me. She deserves some breakfast and she shall have it.'

He went into the house and came back with a handful of crumbs, some warm porridge and some scraps of meat. He scattered them in the Cart and the hen said 'Chuck-chuck-chuck' and walked carefully up one of the shafts and began to pick up crumbs. Tap-tap-tap went her beak, and the old Cart was happy to hear it after so many lonely days.

Then Jim got some bits of wood that were left over when Brownie's shed was made and he nailed them together to make a kind of rough door to the Cart.

'You'd better stay in here while the

snow lasts,' he said to the hen, 'and this will keep the foxes out.' Then he went into the house to boil his egg for breakfast; and the Cart and the hen settled down in each other's company to spend a snug and cheerful Christmas Day.

And that is not the end of the story. The snow melted very soon after Christmas, and one day Jim stood looking at the Cart.

'I've got an idea about you,' he said. 'We'll see tomorrow.'

And next day they did see.

Jim wheeled the old Cart into Brownie's field. He sawed up the shafts and took off the wheels and gave it four short strong little legs to stand on. He tidied up the door and cut a hole in it just large enough for a hen to pop in and out. He nailed up perches and he put a row of nesting-boxes all along one side. Then he tarred the top and painted the sides and legs green, and white-washed it inside. (The hen had to live in Brownie's shed while all this was being done.) And there it stood in the corner of the field, not a worn-out old Cart, but a strong neat chicken-house.

'A happy New Year to you, old fellow,' said Jim when it was finished, and the little brown hen had been popped into her new home. The old Cart felt warm and comfortable inside and out. It certainly was beginning a new, happy year.

It was rather large for one little hen, but when spring was on the way, Jim brought home thirteen brown eggs for her to sit on and she hatched out a brood of fluffy yellow chickens. There were two more broods that summer, and by the time autumn came the Cart was almost as well filled with chickens as it used to be with parcels and people.

It is still standing in the corner of Jim's field. It takes care of the chickens, it shelters them and keeps them snug and warm and dry, it listens to their cluckings and cacklings and crowings and squawkings and their contented little noises when they tell each other tales.

The little brown hen is there too. She is getting old and she seldom lays an egg, but she can still look after a brood of chickens. Jim says she shall never be made into chicken-broth. She shall stay with him and the Cart as long as she lives, in remembrance of the time when she and the Cart kept Christmas together and gave Jim that most surprising present of a warm brown Christmas Egg.

This Story by Elizabeth Clark.

The Cat on the Douvrefell

Have you ever been to Norway, up on the Douvrefell? A traveller once found himself there in winter. The snow was deep and treacherous, the ice worse, and the cold bitter. He was not alone, however. Certainly not! He was leading a big, white bear. He was taking it as a present for the King of Norway. Now, as night fell, he was glad to see the lights of a house and he hurried forward to ask for shelter. A man answered his loud knocking. This man's name was Halvor.

'Will you give me shelter, friend? I do not want to spend the night on the Douvrefell.'

'I cannot. I dare not let you in.'

'Have no fear of the bear,' said the traveller. 'She would never harm you.'

'It's not the bear I fear,' said Halvor.

'Then give me shelter. Surely you won't refuse?'

'I cannot, and you would not wish to stay here this night if you knew the truth.'

The traveller wondered what he could mean. 'Let me in for a little while to warm myself,' he said and Halvor allowed him to enter.

Inside the warm room, the traveller saw a strange sight. The table was loaded with every kind of Christmas food. Delicious smells filled the air and saucepans bubbled on the fire. And yet, Halvor's children huddled in a corner with sad, frightened faces and his wife rattled the pans in haste and fear.

'You are preparing for a good Christmas,' said the traveller.

'Not for us,' Halvor replied.

'It's the same every year,' said the woman. 'We prepare all this and then they come.'

'Who?' asked the traveller.

There was silence.

'The trolls,' said the youngest child.

And so the traveller heard the story. Every year, the trolls came out of the forest. They swarmed around the family, pinching and threatening, and demanding that a great feast should be prepared for Christmas Eve. As each Christmas came, the trolls turned the family out and feasted in the little house, shouting and singing and gobbling all the food that the family had saved for all the year.

'This is a desperate story,' said the man, 'but the bear and I do not fear the trolls. When you leave, I shall make myself a bed in the loft and stay to watch them.'

Halvor and his wife gathered the children, wrapped them up as warmly as they could and hurried out into the night. The traveller settled himself among the hay in the loft and the great bear settled down behind the big stove.

Soon, the traveller heard a distant noise; a squawking and squeaking which grew louder and louder, until through the door flowed a river of trolls.

They were fat and thin, tall and short,
Some had tails and some did not,
Their teeth were yellow,
Their claws were long,
Their hard eyes glittered,
And their manners had gone.

Over the table they swarmed, grabbing at the food, putting their claws in the meat, their feet in the puddings and drinking everything they could.

The man looked down through a crack in the boards and was a little afraid. No wonder Halvor's family had run away. What could they do against so many?

And then, something happened.

There was a great roar from behind the stove and the bear raised herself up and lumbered out.

Then there was a shrieking and a scuffling and a rushing for the door. Crying out in terror, the trolls fought each other to get out, and they ran as fast as they could back to the forest.

No-one saw anything of them for another whole year but, just before Christmas, Halvor was cutting wood when he saw a face peering round a tree. It was one of the trolls.

'Halvor,' he called, 'do you still have your big, white pussy cat?'

'Oh certainly,' replied Halvor, 'and she now has nine kittens, each *almost* as big as herself.'

The troll gave a great shriek and fled back into the forest and Halvor's family never saw any of them ever again.

And when the Christmas feast comes round each year, any stranger from the Douvrefell is welcome at their table.

This story is a re-telling of the Norwegian folk tale by Pat Thomson.

The Rebellious Plum Pudding

Can you imagine how it would be if Christmas weren't allowed? If it were against the law? If you were put in prison for saying, 'Happy Christmas!'

There was such a time.* Gloomy men dressed in black ruled the country without smiling, and Christmas itself was made an outlaw. No services at church. No holidays from work. No feasts or parties. And the town-crier shook his handbell and went through the streets shouting, 'No Christ-mass! No Christ-massing! No Christ-mass by order of the Law!'

Soldiers went from house to house, searching for disobedient Christmassers.

* In 1647 Oliver Cromwell really did ban Christmas. There were riots in the streets and many people were put in prison for defying the Government and the soldiers and celebrating Christmas as they had always done.

A fat goose plucked and ready for cooking, a sprig of holly decorating the fireplace, the sound of carol singing – they were all of them reason enough for the soldiers to break down the door and drag a family away to prison.

As you can imagine, the prisons were *very* full. A lot of people absolutely refused to do without Christmas. They hid their goose in the loft, they sang their carols in the fields and woods or in soft voices when no-one was near, and they whispered to their neighbours through the walls: 'A merry Christmas to you, neighbour!'

But there was one thing that was extremely hard to hide, and that was the smell of plum pudding cooking. Christmas isn't Christmas without a plum pudding. But a pudding takes a long, long time to cook, and there is no keeping that lovely steam under the lid of the pan. So:

'What's that delicious smell creeping

between Mrs Baker's shutters? Plum Pudding! Away with her to prison!'

'What's that delectable smell curling out of the smithy's stable? Plum pudding! Clap him in gaol!'

That's why, when soldiers turned into Market Lane with a crunch-crunch of boots in the snow, Mr Tinker said to his children, 'Quick! Quick! We must hide the pudding! The pudding must be got rid of!'

It was hot, hot, hot. They burnt their fingers getting it out of the pan. They tossed it from one to another: 'Ow, ow! It's hot! Take it!'

'Ow, ow! Here, catch!'

'Hide it! Hide it quick! *Hide the pudding!*'

A rattle at the latch and in burst a Sergeant as big as the giant in the story who could smell the blood of Englishmen: 'Fee! Fie! I smell plum pudding!' he roared. 'I smell *Christmassing*!'

But the Tinkers only blinked at him, all licking their fingers. And they said,

'Plum pudding? Surely not!' as the snow blew in through the open window in little flurries. The Sergeant searched the house from top to bottom, and he smelled that smell in every nook and cranny, till his nose twitched and his mouth watered. But he could not find a pudding.

Meanwhile, out in the garden next-door, a little boy was building a snow-man, a Christmas snowman, when the Tinker's plum pudding came flying out of the window. 'That's just right for the head,' he said when the pudding came rolling by, all coated in snow. And he picked it up and balanced it on top of his snowman and licked his fingers and said, 'Mmm, what a delicious snowball!' Then he put a hat on the top and ran home to tell his mother: 'My snowman's head tastes of cinnamon and sugar!'

But the plum pudding was still hot. It melted the snow underneath it and away it rolled again, out of the garden and down the street.

'A ball!' shouted a milkmaid to her sister, and they put down their buckets and rushed to have a game, a Christmas game of catch. The ball was slippery and heavy and when they licked their fingers they said, 'Mmm, what a delicious football!'

When the plum pudding flew past the window of the schoolroom, everyone inside threw down their slates and chalk and ran out into the streets to join in the game. Even the schoolmaster joined in. It was Christmas, after all, and no-one ought to work at Christmas, Law or no Law.

One thing led to another, and soon there were people dancing and people singing carols, too. The pudding, all lovely and lardy, slipped out of a sticky pair of hands and rolled on up the street, till it came to rest outside the soldiers' barracks.

When the soldiers heard noisy crowds in the streets, saw no-one was working, saw everyone was making holiday, they rattled their pikes and they drew their swords and they rolled out a cannon on to the streets.

'Fee! Fie! You wicked, lawless people!' bellowed the Sergeant. 'Stop this Christmassing or I fire!'

But the crowds only shouted back, 'Happy Christmas! Merry Christmas to you all!' and the soldiers' pikes drooped unhappily.

The Sergeant picked up a cannon ball and put it into the cannon. 'I'm warning you!' he shouted.

'Happy Christmas! Merry Christmas!' shouted back the crowd, as if they were throwing cheeky snowballs.

'I'll count to three, then I'll fire!' bellowed the Sergeant, and his soldiers put their fingers in their ears. 'One!'

'*Two!*' called the crowd. 'You wouldn't dare!'

'Oh but I would . . . *Three!*'

BANG went the cannon.

The street fell silent and filled up with smoke.

Then the smoke cleared.

The crowd stood where it had before . . . picking pieces of cannon ball out of their hair and off their faces and clothes.

'Mmm, what a delicious cannon ball!' they said.

'I do declare I can taste prunes . . .'

'. . . and cinnamon . . .'

'. . . and lard . . .'

'. . . and sugar . . .'

'. . . and orange peel . . .'

'Fee! Fie! Drat!' said the Sergeant and kicked another cannon ball.

But this time it was made of iron and not of prunes at all.

Then the crowd began to laugh, and the soldiers began to laugh, and the cats on the roofs and the rats in the drain joined in, and the birds in their cages, hung in the windows, laughed till they fell off their perches. Someone wheeled out a barrow of oranges, and Mr Tinker pushed up his window and passed out cups of hot punch to women and men, soldiers and children alike.

What could the Sergeant do but hop about with rage and shout, 'You're under arrest! Everyone is under arrest! Everyone everywhere is under arrest!' And the town-crier, passing the end of the street, rang his handbell and called out gloomily, 'No Christ-mass! No Christ-mass! No Christ-mass, by order of the Law!'

Nobody took any notice: they were all much too busy . . . Christmassing.

This story is by Geraldine McCaughrean.

Wil's Tail

Wilmot James Edward Hutchins was the sixth wolf from the left at the school Christmas Concert. When the concert was over everyone said what a good Christmas forest creature he'd been and everyone admired his costume. Wil admired his costume too – especially the tail.

It was a wonderful tail. His mother had made it from the belt of her old fake-fur coat. Wil himself had sewed it to the seat of his favourite corduroy trousers. It was the kind of tail that hung 'just right' and swung 'just right'. It was the kind of a tail with which Wil could slink or jump;

the kind of a tail he could twirl or drape; the kind of a tail he could curl smoothly around him. It had patterns and lines and colours in it that Wil had never even thought about before, and it was softer than anything he'd ever known.

When Wil got home, he hung the wolf mask on his bedroom wall. He put the sweater (his dad's) back in the big dresser drawer. He put the mittens (his sister's) and the moccasins (his mother's) back in the closet where they belonged. But he kept the tail.

The next day was Christmas Eve. Wil helped wrap presents and eat biscuits. When evening came, his family went to a party at the neighbours. Wil's dad wore his smart jeans. Wil's mum wore her party blouse. Wil's sister wore sixteen hair-slides. And Wil wore his tail.

He wore it during supper and he wore it during games and he wore it during carol singing. The neighbours thought it a bit strange, but they were too polite to say anything.

Wil was tired when he got home. He hung up his stocking and rolled into bed. His tail rolled into bed too, all except the tip which hung out over the edge.

On Christmas morning, Wil's family hugged and kissed and opened presents and ate breakfast. They went to the cousins for the day. Wil's dad wore his Christmas tie. Wil's mum wore her Christmas perfume. Wil's sister wore her Christmas brooch and her Christmas socks. Wil wore his Christmas tail.

Aunt Beth nearly had a heart attack when she stepped on it in the kitchen.

On Boxing Day, the family ate leftovers and played 327 games of draughts. The next day they went shopping in the city. Everyone wore their everyday, ordinary clothes. Wil wore his tail.

The tip of it got caught in the escalator of Krumings' department store. A

loud warning bell went off. Two security
people and three maintenance personnel
worked to free the mechanism and every
shopper in the whole store came to see the
boy whose tail had been caught between
the second and third floors.

For the rest of the week Wil stayed at
home with his tail. He repaired it with an
extra piece, so it was longer than ever. He
built a den in the basement. He took long
naps in front of the fire with the cat. And
he waited for New Year's Eve.

On New Year's Eve the family always went skating on Whitefish Lake. Wil was planning on wearing his tail. He could just see himself streaking down the lake in the darkness; the wind rushing smoothly against his face and his tail flying far out behind.

But when New Year's Eve came and he tried to tuck his tail up under his sweater, his mother looked at him and shook her head.

'No,' she said. 'It's dangerous. You'll trip over it and fall and so will everybody else.'

Wil appealed to his father.

'No,' he said. 'It's dangerous. When you go and warm up at the bonfire you're likely to set yourself ablaze.'

'But it's part of me!' said Wil.

His parents did not agree.

'All right,' said Wil. 'I'll wear it but I won't go skating and I won't go near the fire.'

His parents gave in.

Whitefish Lake on New Year's Eve was wonderful. People from all over came to skate and laugh and warm themselves around an enormous bonfire. Wil climbed a little hill between the lake and the river which flowed beyond. He listened to the wonderful sound of skate-blades on ice. He watched skaters passing hockey pucks, turning figures of eight, and playing tick. Just when he could stand it no longer and had decided to take off his tail and put on his skates, he heard shouting behind him.

'Someone's fallen through the river ice!' called the man.

'We can't reach them. A rope. A long scarf. Help! Anyone, please!' called the woman.

Wil thought for only a moment. He reached behind him and pulled with all his might. With a rip his tail came loose. He raced down the slope. The woman took it without a word and disappeared into the darkness.

Wil never did get to go skating on Whitefish Lake that New Year's Eve. By the time all the excitement died down, it was time for his family to go home.

But he did get his tail back. The woman who'd taken it made a special point of bringing it back to him. It was sodden and torn and about four feet longer than it had been to start with. Wil didn't care. His tail had actually saved someone's life!

The tail sits, these days, curled up in a special place, right in the middle of Wil's bedroom shelf – an heroic Christmas tail.

This story is by Hazel Hutchins.

The Christmas Crab Apples

The demon Rubizal lived in the mountain. He was a mischievous one! He played tricks on people. He plagued the wicked and the proud. He put horns on their heads; he gave them pigs' snouts, and asses' tails. But he had a kind heart. Many a poor peasant found money in his pocket, put there by Rubizal. And if he should meet a tired old woman, a long way from home, staggering under a bundle of faggots – puff! Rubizal blew out his cheeks: and the tired old woman found herself seated in comfort by her own fireside, with some of the faggots she had been gathering already blazing on the hearth.

Well, one bitter cold day, just before Christmas, Rubizal gave a hop, skip and jump down from his mountain into the valley. The ground was covered with snow, and trudging along through the snow towards Rubizal came a peasant, very ragged, very thin, and blue with cold. Under his left arm the peasant was carrying a little fir tree, and under his right arm he was carrying a bundle of ivy and holly twigs; and he was looking about him in a worried kind of way.

'What do you seek, my friend?' says Rubizal.

'Oh sir,' says the peasant, 'I am looking for crab apples. Today is Christmas Eve, and after Christmas Eve comes Christmas Day. I am a widower with seven little children, and I would make the time merry for them if I could. I have dug up this little tree; and as you can see, I have some ivy and some holly to decorate it. But I have no money to buy toys or pretty trifles to hang on the tree; and I thought if

100

I could find a few crab apples to gay it up – well, the children would like that. And they could eat the little apples afterwards for a bit of a treat like. Though it would be but a sour feast, when all's said. But there, children will eat most anything . . . But it seems no crab apples grow hereabouts.'

'I know where there is a crab apple tree,' said Rubizal. 'Come!' And he took the peasant into a little wood. In the middle of the little wood was a little crab apple tree. (Well, of course Rubizal had just magicked it there.) The tree was bare of leaves, but there were still small apples hanging on it: not very bright, not very rosy, but still apples.

The peasant, all joyful, set down his bundles, filled his pocket with the little apples, picked up his bundles again.

'Goodbye, and thank you, sir,' says he.

'Goodbye,' says Rubizal. 'A happy Christmas to you!'

'The same to you, sir!' The peasant turned to go home.

'Love to the children!' Rubizal called after him.

'Whose love shall I say, sir?' says the peasant.

'Oh, just a merry old fellow's,' says Rubizal. And he laughs.

The peasant trudged off across the snow. Rubizal gave a jump. There he was, back on his mountain top.

That night, when he had put the children to bed, the peasant filled a box with earth, and planted the Christmas tree in it. He fastened a tallow candle to the top of the tree, and decorated the branches with ivy and holly. Then, very carefully, he threaded some wire through the top of each little apple, and hung the apples on the tree.

'And it does look real festive,' said the peasant to himself, as he stood back to admire his work. 'Though I could wish the apples were a bit more colourful.'

On Christmas morning, when the children saw the tree, they jumped and shouted. They took hands and danced round the tree. And when evening came, and the peasant lit the tallow candle, the ivy glittered and the red holly berries shone, and it seemed that even the little apples looked brighter.

How the children clapped their hands and danced and shouted:

'Oh how pretty! Oh how pretty!
We've got a tree,
A pretty, pretty tree,
We've got a tree, the prettiest of all!'

And there they were, hopping and skipping and turning head over heels.

'But we mustn't forget the gentleman who found the apples,' said the peasant. 'He sent you his love.'

'No, we won't forget him!' cried the children, 'Who was he?'

'Just a merry old fellow,' said the peasant. 'Or so he told me. But the way he spoke, he seemed to me like some great lord.'

'Thank you, thank you, great lord!' shouted the children.

It was a merry evening, though they had nothing but cabbage soup and rye bread for supper.

'And when may we eat the little apples?' asked the children.

'Not till Twelfth Night,' said the peasant. 'That's the day we must take down the tree.'

So, for twelve days, the tree stood in its box of earth in the kitchen. The ivy looked a bit more shrivelled every day, and the holly berries dropped off one by one. The grease from the tallow candle, which of course had burned itself out on Christmas night, lay in patches on the withering leaves: but surely, surely, the little apples were growing every day rosier and bigger! Yes, there was no doubt about it, they *were* rosier, and they *were* bigger. By Twelfth Night they were so big that the branches on the tree bowed under their weight.

'I don't understand it,' muttered the peasant, as he carefully cut the wires and piled the heavy apples on a dish.

'Seems to me half an apple each will be enough for tonight,' says he. 'And they'll last you longer that way.'

'No, no, a whole one each!' cried the children.

'Well, half to begin with, anyway,' said the peasant. And he took a knife and began to halve one of the apples.

The knife cut into the juicy flesh: then it grated on something hard and stuck. What could it be? The peasant turned the apple upside down, and cut again. But again the knife stuck. 'There's something – queer about this apple,' muttered the peasant. And he put down the knife and wrenched the apple in two with his hands.

Oh! Oh! Oh! What do you think?

Out of that apple tumbled six big rubies. Yes, the pips of that apple were precious stones.

'It's – it's witchcraft, it's a Twelfth Night dream, that's what it is!' gasped the peasant. And his hands trembled as he took up another apple and halved it.

It was no dream: the pips of this second apple were shimmering pearls.

And so it went on: the peasant halving apple after apple, and every apple pip a jewel: diamonds, sapphires, pearls, emeralds and rubies. When all the apples were halved, there on the kitchen table lay a gleaming heap of jewels; and even the children, as they munched away at the most delicious fruit they had ever tasted, were awed into silence.

It was a long time before they any of them went to bed. And the peasant couldn't sleep. He turned and tossed, thinking of that pile of jewels. 'It's the fairies up to their Twelfth Night tricks,' said he to himself. 'In the morning all those precious stones will be gone.'

But they weren't gone. The fairies had nothing to do with it. It was a Christmas gift from the demon Rubizal.

So the peasant sold the jewels and bought a farm. Everything prospered with him and his children. No more meagre suppers of cabbage soup and rye bread for them! And each year, before they sat down to their Christmas feast, the happy peasant-turned-farmer gathered his children and his work-people about him, raised his glass, and said, 'Here's a health to the Merry Old Fellow! May we never forget his goodness, whoever he may be!'

And 'A health to the Merry Old Fellow!' cried all in chorus.

Did they hear a chuckling laugh somewhere outside in the snowy darkness? Perhaps they did, perhaps they didn't.

This story is a re-telling of a traditional tale by Ruth Manning-Sanders.

The Mice and the Christmas Tree

Now you shall hear the story about a family of mice who lived behind the larder wall.

Every Christmas Eve, Mother Mouse and the children swept and dusted their whole house with their tails, and for a Christmas tree Father Mouse decorated an old boot with spider's web instead of tinsel. For Christmas presents, the children were each given a little nut, and Mother Mouse held up a piece of bacon fat for them all to sniff.

After that, they danced round and round the boot, and sang and played games till they were tired out. Then Father Mouse would say: 'That's all for tonight! Time to go to bed!'

That is how it had been every Christmas and that is how it was to be this year. The little mice held each other by the tail and danced round the boot, while Granny Mouse enjoyed the fun from her rocking-chair, which wasn't a rocking-chair at all, but a small turnip.

But when Father Mouse said, 'That's all for tonight! Time to go to bed!' all the children dropped each other's tails and shouted: 'No! No!'

'What's that?' said Father Mouse. 'When I say it's time for bed, it's time for bed!'

'We don't want to go!' cried the children, and hid behind Granny's turnip rocking-chair.

'What's all this nonsense?' said Mother Mouse. 'Christmas is over now, so off you go, the lot of you!'

'No, no!' wailed the children, and climbed on to Granny's knee. She hugged them all lovingly. 'Why don't you want to go to bed, my little sugar lumps?'

'Because we want to go upstairs to the big drawing-room and dance round a proper Christmas tree,' said the eldest Mouse child. 'You see, I've been peeping through a crack in the wall and I saw a huge Christmas tree with lots and lots of lights on it.'

'We want to see the Christmas tree and all the lights too!' shouted the other children.

'Oh, but the drawing-room can be a very dangerous place for mice,' said Granny.

'Not when all the people have gone to bed,' objected the eldest Mouse child.

'Oh, do let's go!' they all pleaded.

Mother and Father Mouse didn't know what to say, but they couldn't very well disappoint the children on Christmas Eve.

'Perhaps we could take them up there just for a minute or two,' suggested Mother Mouse.

'Very well,' said Father, 'but follow me closely.'

So they set off. They tiptoed past three tins of herring, two large jars of honey, and a barrel of cider.

'We have to go very carefully here,' whispered Father Mouse, 'not to knock over any bottles. Are you all right, Granny?'

'Of course I'm all right,' said Granny, 'you just carry on. I haven't been up in the drawing-room since I was a little Mouse girl; it'll be fun to see it all again.'

'Mind the trap!' said the eldest Mouse child. 'It's behind that sack of potatoes.'

'I know that,' said Granny; 'it's been there since I was a child. I'm not afraid of that!' And she took a flying leap right over the trap and scuttled after the others up the wall.

'What a lovely tree!' cried all the

children when they peeped out of the hole by the drawing-room fireplace. 'But where are the lights? You said there'd be lots and lots of lights, didn't you? Didn't you?' The children shouted, crowding round the eldest one, who was quite sure there had been lights the day before.

They stood looking for a little while. Then suddenly a whole lot of coloured lights lit up the tree! Do you know what had happened? By accident, Granny had touched the electric switch by the fire-place.

'Oh, how lovely!' they all exclaimed, and Father and Mother and Granny thought it was very nice too. They walked right round the tree, looking at the decorations, the little paper baskets, the glass balls, and the glittering tinsel garlands. But the children found something even more exciting: a mechanical lorry!

Of course, they couldn't wind it up themselves, but its young master had wound it up before he went to bed, to be ready for him to play with in the morning. So when the Mouse children clambered into it, it started off right away.

'Children, children! You mustn't make such a noise!' warned Mother Mouse.

But the children didn't listen; they were having a wonderful time going round and round and round in the lorry.

'As long as the cat doesn't come!' said Father Mouse anxiously.

He had hardly spoken before the cat walked silently through the open door.

Father, Mother, and Granny Mouse all made a dash for the little hole in the skirting but the children were trapped in the lorry, which just went on going round and round and round. They had never been so scared in all their Mouse lives.

The cat crouched under the tree, and every time the lorry passed she tried to tap it with her front paw. But it was going too fast and she missed.

Then the lorry started slowing down. 'I think we'd better make a jump for it and try to get up in the tree,' said the eldest Mouse. So when the lorry stopped they all gave a big jump and landed on the branches of the tree.

One hid in a paper basket, another behind a bulb (which nearly burned him), a third swung on a glass ball, and the fourth rolled himself up in some cotton wool. But where was the eldest Mouse? Oh yes, he had climbed right to the top and was balancing next to the star and shouting at the cat:

> 'Silly, silly cat,
> You can't catch us!
> You're much too fat,
> Silly, silly cat!'

But the cat pretended not to hear or see the little mice. She sharpened her claws on the lorry. 'I'm not interested in catching mice tonight,' she said as if to herself, 'I've been waiting for a chance to play with this lorry all day.'

'Pooh! That's just a story!' said the eldest who was also the bravest. 'You'd catch us quick enough if we came down.'

'No, I wouldn't. Not on Christmas Eve!' said the cat. And she kept her word. When they did all come timidly down, she never moved, but just said: 'Hurry back to your hole, children. Christmas Eve is the one night when I'm kind to little mice. But woe betide you if I catch you tomorrow morning!'

The little mice pelted through that hole and never stopped running till they got to their home behind the larder wall. There were Father and Mother and Granny Mouse waiting in fear and trembling to know what had happened to them.

When Mother Mouse had heard their story she said, 'You must promise me, children, never to go up to the drawing-room again.'

'We promise! We promise!' they all shouted together. Then she made them say after her *The Mouse Law*, which they'd all been taught when they were tiny:

'We promise always to obey
Our parents dear in every way,
To wipe our feet upon the mat
And never, never cheek the cat.

Remember too the awful danger
Of taking money from a stranger;
We will not go off on our own
Or give our mother cause to moan.

Odd bits of cheese and bacon-scraps
Are almost certain to be traps,
So we must look for bigger things
Like loaves and cakes and doughnut-
    rings;

And if these rules we still obey
We'll live to run another day.'

This story is by Alf Prøysen.

Teddy Robinson is a Polar Bear

One day Teddy Robinson sat under the apple-tree looking at a picture book. A little wind rustled the branches over his

head, and soon one or two leaves came fluttering down around him.

'Dear me,' said Teddy Robinson, looking upward, 'this tree seems to be wearing out. Its leaves are falling off.'

Then the wind blew a little stronger and one or two pages blew out of the book (which was an old one) and fluttered away on to the grass.

'There now,' said Teddy Robinson, looking after them, 'this book seems to be wearing out too. It's losing its leaves as well.'

The wind blew stronger still, rustling the leaves and bending the long grass sideways.

'Br-r-r-r!' said Teddy Robinson: 'it's cold. The wind's blowing right through my fur.'

'It's getting thin,' said a sparrow, flying past. 'You should have chosen feathers like me. They wear better.'

'Good gracious, do you mean I'm

wearing out too?' said Teddy Robinson. But the sparrow had gone.

The garden tortoise came creeping slowly past.

'I'm quite worn out myself,' he said. 'I've been tramping round and round looking for a nice warm place to go down under. This pile of leaves looks as good as anywhere. Are you coming down under too, teddy bear? Winter's coming soon and the nights will be growing cold.'

'Oh, no,' said Teddy Robinson, 'I always have a nice warm place down under Deborah's blankets when it's cold at nights.'

'Oh, well, here goes,' said the tortoise, and he began burrowing, nose first, deep into the pile of leaves.

'Anyway,' said Teddy Robinson to himself as he watched the tortoise disappear, 'I wouldn't care to spend the winter down there. Besides, I can't quite remember what it is, but I believe there's something rather nice happens in winter-time. Something worth staying up for.'

So the tortoise stayed buried, and the wind blew colder, and more and more leaves fell off the apple-tree. And because it had grown too cold to play in the garden any more, Teddy Robinson and Deborah played indoors or went for walks instead.

Then one day Teddy Robinson looked out very early in the morning, and saw that all the garden was white with snow. There was snow on the trees, and snow on the roofs of the houses, and thick snowflakes were falling in front of the window. He pressed his nose against the glass and stared out.

'Goodness gracious me,' he said, 'someone's emptied a whole lot of white stuff all over our garden. How different it looks!'

A robin flew down from a nearby tree, scattering snow as he flapped his wings. He hopped on to the window-sill and looked at Teddy Robinson through the window with his head on one side.

'Good morning!' he chirped. 'What do you think of this? Got any crumbs?'

Teddy Robinson nodded at him behind the glass and said, 'Good morning. I'm afraid I haven't any crumbs just now, but I'll ask Deborah at breakfast-time. What's it like out there?'

'Lovely,' said the robin, puffing out his red waistcoat. 'But you wouldn't like it. Snow is all right for white polar bears, but not for brown indoor bears. Well, I must be off now. Don't forget my crumbs!'

He flew away, and Teddy Robinson went on watching the snowflakes falling outside the window and sang to himself:

'There's snow in the garden,
and snow in the air,
and the world's as white
as a polar bear.'

When Deborah woke up, Teddy Robinson showed her the snow as

proudly as if he had arranged it all himself (it felt like his snow because he had seen it first), and she was very pleased. As soon as breakfast was over she put out a saucer full of crumbs on the sill (because he had told her about the robin), and then she put on her coat and boots.

'I'm going to be very busy now,' she said. 'Andrew and I are going to dig away all the snow from people's gates.'

'Can I come?' said Teddy Robinson.

Deborah looked out. 'Yes,' she said, 'it's stopped snowing now. You can sit on the gate-post and watch us.'

So Deborah and Andrew started clearing the snow away from all the front gates while Teddy Robinson sat on his own gate-post and watched them. And after a while it began to snow again. Teddy Robinson got quite excited when he saw the big snowflakes settling on his arms and legs, and he began singing again, happily:

'There's snow in the garden,
and snow in the air,
and the world's as white
as a polar bear.

Snow on the rooftop,
and snow on the tree,
and now while I'm singing
it's snowing on me!'

'Hooray, hooray,' he said to himself. 'Perhaps if it snows on me long enough I shall be all white too. I should love to be a polar bear.'

And it did. It snowed and snowed until Teddy Robinson was quite white all over, with only his eyes and the very tip of his nose showing through.

'I don't believe even Deborah would know me now,' he said, chuckling to himself. And it seemed as if he was right, because when Deborah came running back for dinner Teddy Robinson kept

quite still and didn't say a word, and she ran right past him into the house without recognizing him.

'This *is* fun!' said Teddy Robinson. 'All this snow must be the nice thing I'd forgotten about, that happens in wintertime. It was worth staying up for.' And he felt sorry for the poor old tortoise who was down at the bottom of the pile of leaves and missing it all.

126

How surprised Deborah will be when she comes back and finds I've turned into a polar bear, he thought.

But Deborah didn't come back because after dinner she made a snowman in the back garden and forgot all about him. Teddy Robinson didn't know this, but he was having such a jolly time being a polar bear all by himself on top of the gate-post that he didn't notice what a long time she was.

First the Next Door Kitten came picking her way along the wall, shaking her paws at every step. She looked at Teddy Robinson as if she didn't quite believe in him, and they had a little conversation.

'Who are you?'

'I'm a polar bear.'

'Why aren't you at the North Pole?'

'I came to visit friends here.'

'Oh!'

Then Toby the dog (who belonged to Deborah's friend Caroline) came galloping up. He was a rough and noisy dog who liked chasing cats and barking at teddy bears. The Next Door Kitten jumped quickly over the wall into her own garden, but Teddy Robinson kept quite still until Toby was sniffing round the gate-post. Then he let out a long, low growl.

Toby jumped and barked loudly. Teddy Robinson growled again.

'Who's that?' barked Toby.

'Gr-r-r, a polar bear. Run like mad before I catch you!'

Toby looked round quickly, but couldn't see anyone.

'Go on, *run*,' said Teddy Robinson in his big polar bear's voice. 'RUN!'

Toby didn't wait for any more. With a yelp which sounded more like Help! he ran off up the road as fast as he could go.

'Well, I'll never be frightened of *him* again,' said Teddy Robinson.

Then the robin flew down from the hedge and perched on the gate-post beside him and cocked a bright eye at him.

'Hallo,' he chirped. 'Who are you?'

'I'm a polar bear.'

The robin looked at him sideways, hopped round to his other side, and looked again. Then Teddy Robinson sneezed.

'You're not,' said the robin. 'You're the brown bear who lives in the house. I saw you this morning. I told you then this snow isn't right for an indoor bear like you. You'll catch cold. But thanks for my crumbs. I'll look for some more at tea-time. I hope you'll be having toast? I like toast.' And before Teddy Robinson could answer he had flown off again over the white roofs of the houses.

It grew very quiet in the road. People's footsteps made no sound in the snow and it seemed as if the world was wrapped in cotton wool. Teddy Robinson was beginning to feel cold. Soon one or two lights went on in the houses, and in a window opposite he could see a lady getting tea ready.

'I wonder if she is making toast,' he said to himself, and felt a little colder.

Then he began thinking about the tortoise tucked away in the big pile of leaves.

'He must be quite cosy down there,' he said, and he thought of the leaves all warm and crunchy and smelling of toast, and almost wished he had gone down too.

'But of course, if I had, I should never have been able to be a polar bear sitting on a gate-post,' he said; and to keep his spirits up he began singing a polar bear song:

'Ice
is nice,
and so
is snow.
Ice
is nice
when cold winds blow—'

but the words were so cold that they made him sneeze again.

'Never mind,' said Teddy Robinson bravely, 'I'll think of something else. I'll make up a little song called The Polar Bear on the Gate-Post.'

But it was hard to find anything to rhyme with gate-post, and the more he thought about it, the more he found himself saying 'plate' instead of 'gate', and 'toast' instead of 'post', so that in the end, instead of singing about a Polar Bear on a Gate-Post, he was singing about an Indoor Bear on a Plate of Toast, which wasn't what he'd meant at all.

'But it *would* be nice and warm sitting on a plate of toast,' he said to himself. And then suddenly he thought, Of course! *That's* the nice thing that happens in winter-time. It's not snow at all. It's toast for tea!

And at that moment the robin came flying back chirping, 'Toast for tea! Toast for tea! Is it ready?'

When he found the saucer empty on the window-sill and poor Teddy Robinson still sitting in the snow, with an icicle on the end of his nose, the robin was quite worried.

'They must have forgotten you,' he said. 'I'll remind them.' And he flew up to the window and beat his wings hard on the glass. Then he flew back to Teddy Robinson.

Deborah came to the window and looked out.

'Oh, Mummy!' she called. 'There's the robin, and he's sitting on – he's sitting on – why, it's Teddy *Robinson*, all covered in snow and looking just like a polar bear! And the robin's sitting on his head.'

'Oh, don't they look pretty!' said Mummy. 'Just like a Christmas card!'

Then Teddy Robinson was brought in and made a great fuss of. And afterwards, while Mummy made the toast for tea and Deborah put out fresh crumbs for the rob-in, he sat in front of the fire and bubbled and mumbled and simmered and sang,

just like a kettle when it's coming up to
the boil:

'*Tea and toast,*
toast and tea,
the tea for you
and the toast for me.
How nice to be a warm, brown bear
toasting in a fireside chair.'

When bedtime came Teddy Robinson's
fur was still not quite dry, so Mummy said he had better stay downstairs
and she would bring him up later. So
Deborah went off to bed, and Mummy
went off to cook grown-up supper, and
Teddy Robinson toasted and dozed in the
firelight and was very cosy indeed.

Then Daddy came home, puffing and
blowing on his fingers and stamping the
snow off his shoes. He took a little parcel out of the pocket of his big overcoat
and gave it to Mummy. Inside was a

fairy doll, very small and pretty, with a white-and-silver dress, and a silver crown and wand.

'Oh, a new fairy for the Christmas tree!' said Mummy, standing her upon the table. 'How pretty! That is just what we need. Now come and have supper, it's all ready.'

So Daddy and Mummy went off to their supper, leaving the fairy doll on the table and Teddy Robinson in front of the fire.

'A new fairy for the Christmas tree,' said Teddy Robinson to himself. 'The *Christmas* tree. I'd forgotten all about it,' and his fur began to tingle. He suddenly remembered how the Christmas tree looked, with toys and tinsel all over it, and little coloured lights, and a pile of exciting little parcels all round it. And he remembered himself, sitting close beside it in his best purple dress, trying to see if any of the parcels were for him, without looking as if he was looking. And then he remembered how there always was a parcel for him, and how it was always just what he wanted.

'Of course!' he said, '*that's* the nice thing that happens in winter-time, that I'd forgotten about. It's not snow (though that's very nice), and it's not toast for tea (though that's nicer still), but it's Christmas, and that's nicest of all!'

There was a rustling over his head and the fairy doll whispered in a tiny little voice, 'Would you like a wish, teddy bear? If you like you can have one now. It will be the very first wish I've ever given anyone.'

Teddy Robinson said, 'Thank you,' then he thought hard, then he sighed happily.

'It seems a terrible waste of a wish,' he said, 'but I don't think I've anything left to wish for. I'll wish you and everyone else a very merry Christmas.'

And that is the end of the story about how Teddy Robinson was a Polar Bear.

This story is by Joan G. Robinson.

While Shepherds Watched

'We're going to do a Nativity Play,' said Charlie. 'Just us, not Sir's class, and I'm going to be a shepherd.'

'Sir says it ought to be us doing the play because we're older,' said Lucinda, 'but Miss Clarke thought of it first, so it has to be you.'

'It'll be all right,' said Charlie. 'Sir's going to be knocked back when he sees it.'

The Lower Juniors worked very hard at their play. They all wanted to show Sir what they could do. Tim was St Joseph and his father made a stable with doors that opened and closed. When Tim and

Jennifer Muller, who played Mary, had been settled in the stable by Robert the innkeeper, they could close the doors and the audience could forget about them until the time came for the stable to be opened again for the shepherds to visit the newborn baby.

Tim's sister Annalise, who had come up from Mrs Bray's class into the Lower Juniors that term, was an angel and Miranda Jefferson was the Black King. Her family had moved into the village a month before. They had come over from the United States, so that Miranda's mother could teach drama at the university outside Burracombe. Her father had come too, because he wrote detective stories and said it didn't matter where he wrote them so long as he was left in peace. The other member of the family was baby Dominic, who was six months old. Mrs Jefferson made herself very useful organizing a group of mothers to make clothes for the play.

'It's going to be super,' Charlie announced one tea-time. 'Just you wait.'

'It had better be,' said Lucinda. 'Sir's wishing we were doing it after all.'

'It's too late now,' said Charlie. 'There's only a week to go. What's he on about?'

'Mrs Jefferson's gone and contacted the local television people, and they're sending a cameraman on the day to take pictures. Sir doesn't know whether to be pleased or not. He doesn't know whether you lot are to be trusted not to let the school down.'

'Don't worry,' Mrs Robinson comforted her. 'It won't be broadcast live. If they don't like it, they won't put it out. They don't show everything they film.'

Charlie almost burst with indignation. 'They jolly well are going to show *us*,' he said.

The Lower Juniors were so excited at the thought of the television cameras that even Miss Clarke was a bit worried about how they would react on the day. Charlie lay awake at nights thinking about it. The play wasn't bad. They had Mrs Jefferson's super costumes and Mr Crossman's stable. He talked to Miranda about it and she told him to quit worrying, but Charlie insisted that it still needed something to make it extra special so that people would remember it for years to come. The great idea came to him on the day of the dress rehearsal. They were doing it on the stage of the village hall. When the shepherds reached the stable, Charlie had to give a sheepskin to Tim, who put it over the baby in the manger.

'Soppy-looking baby,' muttered Charlie, as he handed the skin over and watched Tim tuck it round the stiff doll with staring eyes that Annie Thomas had brought to be Baby Jesus.

'What we want is a real baby,' said Charlie to some of the others when the rehearsal was over.

'Where'd we get one from?' asked Jennifer.

'There must be heaps of babies about,' said Charlie.

'There's a baby in the bungalow opposite the garage,' said Annalise.

'It's too big and its nose runs and it's a horrible baby,' said Tim.

'There's Dominic,' said Miranda.

Everyone looked at her. They were all thinking the same thing but nobody liked to say it. At last Tim spoke. 'He's the wrong colour,' he said.

'How do you know?' asked Miranda. 'Have you ever seen Jesus, Tim Crossman? How do you know he wasn't black?'

'He just wasn't,' said Tim. 'Jesus was a white man.'

'That's because white men wrote the Bible, I guess,' said Miranda. 'If a black man had written the Bible, Jesus would have been black.'

'No he wouldn't,' said Jennifer. 'He was a Jew, wasn't he? He came from Palestine, where Israel is today. What colour are the people who live there?'

Nobody knew.

'Let's watch the news tonight,' said Jennifer. 'There's been trouble with bombs going off. If there are pictures from Israel we can see what colour the people are.'

That evening more children than usual watched the television news bulletins, and the next day, everyone agreed that people from Israel were darker than British people but not as dark as Miranda.

'So a white baby's just as wrong as a black baby,' said Miranda. 'We haven't got one the right colour, so I'll get Dominic.'

'How do we get hold of him?' asked Tim. 'You can't just walk into your house and hoik him out.'

'Yes I can,' said Miranda. 'Dad's baby-sitting while Mum comes to the play, and when Dad's writing a book, he doesn't notice whether it's Dominic or a baby elephant in the cot.'

'But suppose he does notice?' asked Tim. 'We don't want him dialling 999.'

'I'll leave a note in Domie's cot to say he's with me,' Miranda promised.

The television men moved in on the day of the play. There was a sound recordist, a cameraman and an interviewer. They talked and joked with the children while they were putting on their costumes and took pictures of them while they were getting ready for the play. At half past two, they joined the audience and the performance began. To get people in the right mood, the Top Juniors sang some carols, and while Miss Clarke accompanied them on the piano in the hall and Mrs Patterson, who had come to help backstage, was trying to keep the Lower Juniors quiet, Miranda slipped out to fetch Dominic. She returned with a sleeping bundle in her arms just as Mr Beezy the caretaker was pulling back the curtains for the Nativity Play.

'Here he is,' she whispered to Tim and Jennifer, who were waiting in the wings.

'Quiet now, dears,' said Mrs Patterson, who had no idea what was going on. 'Mr Beezy's drawing the curtain.'

The play began. There was some music from the piano, and Mary and Joseph came on looking for somewhere to stay. The innkeeper and his wife led them to Mr Crossman's stable, and Robert carefully closed the doors. While the shepherds acted their scene, they could hear whispering behind the stable doors and guessed that Dominic was being put into the crib. Behind the doors, sheltered from the lights, Dominic slept, and Tim and Jennifer waited anxiously for the moment when the stable would be opened. But when Robert drew back the doors, Dominic slept on.

'It's going to be OK,' breathed Tim, and then turned himself into St Joseph, who greeted the shepherds and thanked

them for coming. He took the sheepskin from Charlie and tucked it round
Dominic. The audience smiled; it was
a nice idea. Then they gasped. Dominic
was already hot, and a sturdy black leg
came up to kick at the rug. The sheepskin
slipped to one side and a white knitted
bootee shot off his foot and flew across
the stage. Dominic gurgled, kicked and
waved his arms at Jennifer. Charlie was
delighted.

Miranda peered anxiously from the
wings. Would Tim have the sense to leave
the sheepskin where it was? 'Leave it,' she
whispered. 'He doesn't want it.' But Tim
didn't hear. He decided that St Joseph
wasn't the sort of person to put up with
nonsense from a baby, and he tucked the
rug firmly over Dominic's legs. Dominic
opened his mouth and started to bawl his
head off. He made so much noise that he
drowned the words the shepherds were
supposed to say.

Miss Clarke half rose from her seat at

the piano. Sir clapped a hand to his head and told himself that it wasn't happening. Some of the audience at the back of the hall stood up to get a better view, Mrs Jefferson started moving out of her seat, and the cameraman brought his camera right up to the stage.

Then Miranda made up her mind. She came on, bringing the other two Kings with her. It was almost time for them to be on anyway and no-one could hear the shepherds' last speeches through that awful racket. She went straight to the crib and lifted out her baby brother, who stopped crying at once. Holding him in her arms, she turned to Mary. 'I see your baby is giving you trouble,' she said. 'You just let me have him, ma'am. I have children of my own at home. I know what it's like.'

The audience and the rest of the cast held its breath as Tim rose splendidly to the occasion. 'Thank you, sir,' he replied. 'You see, Mary isn't used to babies, this is her first.'

'Thank you,' said Jennifer faintly, wondering how they were ever to get back to the play as Miss Clarke had written it. 'Is that some gold you have there?'

'Gold I bring for the little King,' said Miranda, getting back into her part and using the words she had learnt. She glared at the other two Kings, who had been looking on in amazement, and this reminded them that they had words to say as they presented their gifts to Mary and Joseph. Then Annalise entered to tell them to avoid Herod's court and go home by another way and the play came to an end. As the cast lined up to bow, Miranda put the now gurgling Dominic into Jennifer's arms and stepped back to take her place with the other Kings.

The audience clapped and cheered and the television crew was delighted at the sudden turn of events. 'You'll be seeing yourselves on Monday,' they promised as they left.

Dominic was restored to his mother

while the cast changed and then went to join their parents for tea and cakes at the back of the hall. Charlie was jubilant. 'Couldn't have been better,' he said.

Then Lucinda appeared. 'Sir is looking for you,' she told him.

'Oh, gosh.' Charlie suddenly realized how grown-ups might look at it – bringing a live baby on to the stage without telling anybody. He wormed his way through the crowd and stood in front of Sir.

'You and Miranda ought to be punished for this,' Sir began. 'But as usual I am outvoted and you have a band of loyal supporters, including the baby's father.'

'His father!' gasped Charlie.

A tall man stepped forward. 'Yes,' he said. 'I'm Dominic's father. I was in the bedroom when Miranda came in, and she told me what she was going to do. It seemed like a good idea to me, so I said go ahead.'

'I'm sorry he yelled so much,' said

Mrs Jefferson. 'But he wasn't bad for his first acting part.'

Sir cast his eyes towards the ceiling. 'What can I do,' he asked, 'when the whole family is on their side?'

'There's nothing you can do,' said Mrs Robinson, who was standing beside him. 'Charlie will always be Charlie, and now he's been joined by Miranda, anything could happen.'

'Well, thank goodness the holidays begin on Tuesday,' said Mr McKay. 'Whatever happens in the next three weeks, it won't be my responsibility.'

This story is by Sylvia Woods.

The Glass Peacock

Annar-Mariar lived in a queer old alley in one of the queerest and oldest parts of London. Once this part had been a real village all by itself, looking down from its hill upon the fields and lanes that divided it from the town. Then gradually the town had climbed the hill, the fields were eaten up by houses, and the lanes suffered that change which turned them into streets. But the hill was so steep, and the ways were so twisty, that even the town couldn't swallow the village when it got to the top. It was too much trouble to make broad roads of all the funny little narrow turnings, so some of them were left much as they were, and one of these was the alley where Annar-Mariar lived. It ran across from one broad road to another, a way for walkers, but not for carts and cars. The two big roads met at a point a little farther on, so there was no need to turn Annar-Mariar's alley into a thoroughfare for traffic, and it remained a paved court, with poor irregular dwellings and a few humble shops on each side. Being paved, and out of the way of motors, it became a natural playground for the children who lived in it; and even from the other alleys near by children came to play in Mellin's Court. The organ-grinder, making his way from one big road to another, sometimes made it across Mellin's Court. One day, as he was passing, a group of children were clustered round the little sweetstuff shop that sold bright sweets in hap'orths, or even farthings-worths. The shop had an old bow window nearly touching the pavement – it came down about as far

as a little girl's skirt, and went up about as high as a man's collar. To enter the shop, you went down three steps into a dim little room. None of the children had any farthings that day except Annar-Mariar, and *she* had a whole penny. Her little brother Willyum was clinging to the hand that held the penny, and telling her all the things he liked best in the jars in the window. He knew his Annar-Mariar, and so did the other children who were not her brothers and sisters.

'I like the lickerish shoe-strings,' said Willyum.

'*I* like the comfits with motters on,' said Mabel Baker.

'And I like the pink and white mouses,' said Willyum.

'Them bulls' eyes is scrumpchous,' observed Doris Goodenough.

'And the chocklit mouses,' continued Willyum, 'and I like them long stripey sticks, and them chocklit cream bars with pink inside.'

'Peardrops,' murmured Kitty Farmer.

'And white inside too,' said Willyum.

While Annar-Mariar was puzzling and puzzling how to make her penny go round she saw the organ-grinder, and cried, 'Oo! An orgin!' The other children turned. 'Ply us a chune, mister!' they cried. 'Ply us a chune!' The organ-grinder shook his head. 'No time today,' he said. Annar-Mariar went up to the organ-grinder and smiled at him, plucking his coat.

'Do ply 'em a chune to dance to,' she said, and held out her penny. It was Annar-Mariar's nice smile, and not her penny, that won the day. Annar-Mariar was quite an ordinary-looking little girl until she smiled. Then you felt you would do anything for her. This was because Annar-Mariar would always do anything for anybody. It came out in her smile, and got back at her, so to speak, by winning her her own way. All day long Mellin's Court was calling her name. 'Annar-Mariar! Johnny's bin and hurted hisself.' 'Annar-Mariar! Come quick! Bobby and Joan is fighting somethink orful!' 'Annar-Mariar, boo-hoo! I've broke my dolly!' Or it might be an older voice. 'Annar-Mariar! Jest keep an eye on baby for me while I go round the corner.' Yes, everybody knew that Annar-Mariar would always be ready to heal the hurt, and soothe the quarrel, and mend the doll, and mind the baby. She would not only be ready to, but she could *do* it; because everybody did what she wanted them to.

So the organ-grinder refused her penny, and stopped and played three tunes for her smile; and the children got a jolly dance for nothing, and Willyum got a pair of licorice shoe-strings for a farthing. The rest of Annar-Mariar's penny went in Hundreds and Thousands, and every child licked its finger and had a dip. There wasn't a fingerful over for Annar-Mariar, so she tore open the tiny bag and licked it off with her tongue.

After that the organ-grinder made a point of cutting across Mellin's Court on his rounds, stopping outside the Rat-Catcher's, where it was at its broadest, to play his tunes; and the children gathered there and danced, and sometimes he got a copper for his kindness, but whether he did or not made no difference. He always came once a week.

Christmas drew near, and the little shops in Mellin's Court began to look happy. The sweetstuff shop had a Fairy Doll in white muslin and tinsel in the middle of the window, and some paper festoons and cheap toys appeared among the glass bottles. At the greengrocer's, a sort of glorified open stall which overflowed into the courtyard, evergreens and pineapples appeared, and on one magic morning Christmas trees. The grocery window at the corner had already blossomed into dates and figs and candied fruits, and blue-and-white jars of ginger; and the big confectioner's in the High Street had in the window, as well as puddings in basins, a Christmas Cake a yard square – a great flat frosted 'set piece', covered with robins, windmills, snow babies, and a scarlet Santa Claus with a sled full of tiny toys. This cake would presently be cut up and sold by the pound, and you got the attractions on top 'as you came' – oh lucky, lucky buyer-to-be of the Santa Claus sled! The children of Mellin's Court were already choosing their favourite toys and cakes and fruits from the rich windows, and Annar-Mariar and Willyum chose like all the rest. Of course, they never *thought* they could have the Fairy Queen, the Christmas tree, the big box of sugary fruits, or the marvellous cake – but how they *dreamed* they could! As Christmas drew nearer, smaller hopes of what it would actually bring began to take shape in the different homes. Bobby's mother had *told* him he'd better hang his stocking up on Christmas Eve 'and see'. That meant something. And the Goodenoughs were going to be sent a hamper. And Mabel Baker was going to be taken to the Pantomime! And the Jacksons were all going to their Granny's in Lambeth for a party. And this child and that had so much, or so little, in the Sweet Club.

And as Christmas drew nearer, it became plainer and plainer to Annar-

Mariar that this year, for one reason or another, Christmas wasn't going to bring her and Willyum anything. And it didn't. Up to the last they got *their* treat from the shop-windows, and did all their shopping there. Annar-Mariar never stinted her Christmas Window-shopping.

'What'll *you* 'ave, Willyum? I'll 'ave the Fairy Queen, I think. Would you like them trains?'

'Ss!' said Willyum. 'And I'd like the Fairy Queen.'

'Orl right. You 'ave her. I'll 'ave that music box.'

At the confectioner's: 'Shall we 'ave a big puddin' for us both, or a little puddin' each, Willyum?'

'A big puddin' each,' said Willyum.

'Orl right. And them red crackers with the gold bells on, and I'll tell 'em to send the big cake round too, shall I?'

'Ss!' said Willyum, 'and I'll 'ave the Farver Crismuss.'

'Orl right, ducks. You can.'

And at the grocer's Willyum had the biggest box of candied fruits, and at the greengrocer's the biggest pineapple. He agreed, however, to a single tree – the biggest – between them, and under Annar-Mariar's lavish disregard of money there was plenty of everything for them both, and for anybody who cared to 'drop in' on Christmas Day.

It came, and passed. The windows began to be emptied of their attractions for another year. Mabel Baker went to the Pantomime, and told them all about it. Annar-Mariar dreamed of it for nights; she thought she was a very lucky girl to have a friend who went to the Panto.

Life went on. The New Year rang itself in. At dusk, on Twelfth Night, Annar-Mariar knelt on the paving-stones in Mellin's Court and renewed a chalk game that had suffered during the day. She happened to be the only child about, a rare occurrence there.

She heard footsteps go by her, but

did not look up at once; only, as they passed, she became aware of a tiny tinkling accompaniment in the footsteps. Then she did look up. A lady was going slowly along the alley with something astonishing in her hands.

'Oo!' gasped Annar-Mariar.

The lady stopped. What she was carrying was a Christmas tree, quite a little tree, the eighteenpenny size, but such a *radiant* little tree! It was glittering and twinkling with all the prettiest fantasies in glass that the mind of Christmas had been able to invent, little gas lamps and candlesticks, shining balls of every colour, a scarlet-and-silver Father Christmas, also in glass, chains and festoons of gold and silver beads, stars, and flowers, and long clear drops like icicles; birds, too, in glass, blue and yellow birds, seeming to fly, and one, proudest and loveliest of all, a peacock, shimmering in blue and green and gold, with a crest and long, long tail of fine spun glass, like silk.

'Oo!' gasped Annar-Mariar. 'A Christmas tree!'

The lady did an undreamed-of thing. She came straight up to Annar-Mariar and said, 'Would you like it?'

Annar-Mariar gazed at her, and very slowly smiled. The lady put the tinkling tree into her hands.

'This,' she said, 'was for the first little girl that said Oo! and you're the little girl.'

Annar-Mariar began to giggle – she

simply *couldn't* say 'Thank you!' She could only giggle and giggle. Her smile, however, turned her giggling into the loveliest laughter, and seemed to be saying 'Thank you,' on top of it. The lady laughed, and disappeared from Mellin's Court.

Willyum appeared in her place. 'Wot's that?'

' 'Ts a Crismuss tree. A lidy give it to me.'

Willyum scampered screaming down the alley. 'Annar-Mariar's gotter Crismuss tree wot a lidy give 'er!'

The crowd collected. They gathered round the tree, looking, touching, admiring, and the 'Oos!' came thick and fast.

'Oo! see ol' Farver Crismuss!'

'Oo! see them birds, like flying, ain't they?'

'Do the lamps reely light, Annar-Mariar?'

'Oo! ain't that flower loverly!'

'Wotcher goin' to do wiv it, Annar?'

'I shall keep it by my bed ternight,'

said Annar-Mariar, 'and termorrer I shall give a party.'

Longing glances flew about her.

'Can I come, Annar-Mariar?'

'Can I?'

'Can I?'

'Let *me* come, won't yer, Annar?'

'You can all come,' said Annar-Mariar.

That night, that one blissful night, the little tree in all its gleaming beauty shone upon Annar-Mariar's dreams – waking dreams, for she hardly slept at all. She kept looking at it, and feeling it when she couldn't see it, running her finger along the glassy chains, outlining the fragile flowers and stars, stroking the silken tail of the miraculous peacock. Tomorrow night, she knew, her tree would be harvested, but she thought her own particular fruit might be the peacock. If so, he could sit on the tree beside her bed for ever, and every night she could stroke his spun-glass tail.

The morrow came. The party was

held after tea. Every child in Mellin's Court took home a treasure. Willyum wanted the Father Christmas, and had him. The other children did not ask for the peacock. Somehow they knew how *much* Annar-Mariar wanted it, and recognized that off *her* tree she should have what she prized most. Little Lily Kensit *did* murmur, when her turn came, 'I'd like the peac—' But her big brother clapped his hand over her mouth, and said firmly, 'Lil'd like the rose, Annar-Mariar. Look, Lil, it's got a dimond in the middle.'

'Oo!' said Lil greedily.

So when the party was over, and the little empty tree was dropping its dried needles on the table, Annar-Mariar was left in possession of the magical bird whose tail she had touched in her dreams.

When she came to put Willyum to bed, he was sobbing bitterly.

'Wot's the matter, ducks?'

'I broke my Farver Crismuss.'

'Oh, Willyum . . . you never.'

'Yus, I did.' Willyum was inconsolable.

'Don't cry, ducks.'

'I want your peacock.'

'Orl right. You can. Don't cry.'

Annar-Mariar gave Willyum her peacock. He sobbed himself to sleep, clutching it, and in the night he dropped it out of bed. Annar-Mariar heard it 'go' as she lay beside her little empty tree. All night long the pungent scent of the Christmas tree was in her nostrils, and the tiny crickle of its dropping needles in her ears.

And in the room of every other child in Mellin's Court some lovely thing was set above its dreams, a bird, or flower, or star of coloured glass; to last perhaps a day, a week, a few months, or a year – or even many years.

This story is by Eleanor Farjeon.